dis ... essence of

leadership

discovering the essence of

leadership

TONY MANNING

ZEBRA

Published by Zebra Press
an imprint of Struik Publishers
(a division of New Holland Publishing (South Africa) (Pty) Ltd)
PO Box 1144, Cape Town, 8000
New Holland Publishing is a member of the Johnnic Publishing Group

First published 2002

10 9 8 7 6 5 4 3 2

Publication © Zebra Press 2002
Text © Tony Manning 2002

PUBLISHING MANAGER: Marlene Fryer
MANAGING EDITOR: Robert Plummer
COVER AND TEXT DESIGNER: Natascha Adendorff
TYPESETTER: Natascha Adendorff

Set in 10 pt on 14 pt Palatino

Reproduction by Hirt & Carter (Cape) (Pty) Ltd
Printed and bound by CTP Book Printers

ISBN 1 86872 659 2

www.zebrapress.co.za

Log on to our photographic website www.imagesofafrica.co.za for an African experience

For Sandy,
who stood steadfastly beside me
while I discovered
my self.

CONTENTS

GUIDEPOSTS   11

INTRODUCTION   **13**

Confusion about a critical function   15

Promises, promises   17

Many paths   18

Great through others   19

The extended enterprise   21

The scorecard   21

The "X factor": followers   24

The gift of winning   25

The payoff   26

1   **THE PERSON**   **27**

Managers vs. leaders   28

Unleash the magic   30

Born or made?   31

Not all equal   32

Out of the blue   34

Suddenly ... Sir Rudy   35

Give me a break!   36

Your potential   38

Who are you? 39

Footprints in the sand 42

The danger of hubris 43

Keep your feet on the ground 46

Remember the golden rule 47

2 **THE WORK OF LEADERS** **49**

What followers expect 52

Two frames 53

What you see and say 56

Get real 57

Facts and assumptions 59

Basics and breakthroughs 61

Building "strategic IQ" 62

Expectations and performance 64

The person or the place? 65

The culture trap 66

Change on the run 68

Climate for action 68

Magic in meaning 70

Trust 71

3 **ON BEING EFFECTIVE** **73**

Action on purpose 74

"The hill" 74

Your point of view 76

Ground rules 78

Four modes of operating 79

The second right answer   82

The finite resource   83

Leaders as teachers   84

Lifelong learning   86

Pause to reflect   87

4   TOMORROW'S LEADERS   **89**

Insiders or outsiders?   89

Selecting against the odds   90

Settling in   94

Decision time!   95

CONCLUSION   **97**

THE PRACTICES   99

REFERENCES   101

GUIDEPOSTS

1. Leadership is a gift that you are given, and that you, in turn, give to others.

2. To lead is to achieve a specific purpose through others.

3. Leaders need followers. They make you or break you. Treat them as assets not asses, and they will commit themselves to your success.

4. Your effectiveness is determined by the way you frame the world for yourself and others, and the way you manage the arena in which your people work.

5. Meaning is the ultimate motivator.

6. Strategic conversation is the ultimate leadership tool. It defines your purpose, goals, priorities, and actions, and involves your team in creating the future.

7. Change actions, and you change minds.

8. "Strategic IQ" comes from facing challenges, not from sitting at a desk in a classroom.

9. To be effective, you have to build an effective, robust organization. Stay focused on that goal, and all else will fall into place.

10. Over-communicate everything. Be clear. Be consistent. Be persistent.

INTRODUCTION

"The Businessman of the Century was the builder of an industry that transformed the very land we live on, the first to create a mass market as well as the means to satisfy it, as great an entrepreneur as we've ever seen. He was a provincial and a curmudgeon; a man with all the prejudices of his time, who had as well the kind of genius that endures. He is Henry Ford."[1]

*Thomas A. Stewart, Alex Taylor III, Peter Petre and Brent Schlender,
"The Businessman of the Century,"* Fortune, *22 November 1999*

Throughout history, there have been calls for leadership. It's always been a big deal. Today, it's more important than ever to society and its institutions. Things are changing at an astonishing pace. Turbulence is normal. Surprise is everywhere, and a 24×7 reality. The challenges are huge. Yet, by all accounts, there are too few leaders to go around.

The first year of the twenty-first century was a turning point for humankind. Terror attacks on the United States of America, economic pressures, and the Enron/Andersen imbroglio thrust leaders into the spotlight. They were always important, but now they are needed as never before. At the same time, questions about ethics, values, corporate governance, pay, and performance have come to haunt them.

Leaders have to make their businesses competitive. That's getting harder by the minute. For most companies across the globe, the first wave of efficiency gains is past. They've cut jobs. They've outsourced many functions. They've put red lines through research and development, training, promotions, travel, and just about everything else. Cutting further will be suicidal.

But sales and margins are under pressure. Customers are skittish and disloyal. Competition is fierce. Growth is elusive.

Contrary to what many people think, "fair weather" leaders are not two-a-penny. Those who can lead in foul weather are even rarer. Today, there's seldom a break in the clouds.

For all these reasons, leadership is a headline issue, along with strategy and change management. Yet, while they're seen as separate "disciplines," it's clear that they're intertwined. Leaders must be strategists and change masters, for they are ultimately measured by their ability to choose the right things to do, and get them done.

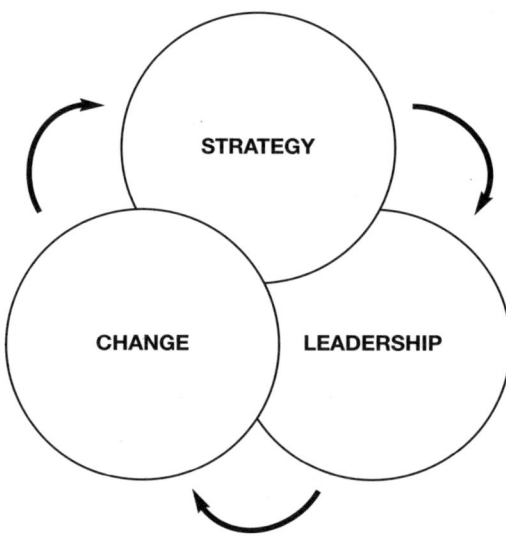

Figure I-I *A holistic view*

This book is a companion to my previous one, *Making Sense of Strategy*,[2] and builds on many of the ideas I wrote about there. While the focus here is on business leadership, the principles apply equally to leaders in any organization. Again, I've tried to be brief, to let you get the information you need fast.

Confusion about a critical function

Leadership is a mystery. It's a role and it's work. We know a great deal about leadership, but not enough to make it a discipline. We think we know what to look for in future leaders, but we don't know how to find it. We know what we expect from our leaders, but not how to produce them. We look up to them, and down on them.

I've worked with many leaders, and observed even more, and they're all different. Some are *boringly* consistent and predictable; others are real loose cannons. Some are correct in everything they do; others wing it all the way. Some are politeness personified; others are pigs.

It's tempting to say that all the good ones are consistent, predictable, correct, and polite, while the less effective ones aren't. But that wouldn't be true. It takes all types to make the world.

Much of what's said about leadership is interesting, but unhelpful. Much of the advice on how to be a leader sounds good, but doesn't work. Much of what we think we know about identifying and developing tomorrow's leaders is pure fiction. (For example, how do you explain the fact that psychometric testing is so popular, yet executive failure is so common?)

A subject this big is fertile ground for "experts." Here's what you'll get if you listen to them:

- Most organizations are over-managed and under-led.
- Everyone's a leader – or *could* be, with the right training.
- There are leaders at every level – or *should* be.
- Leadership is an art.
- Leadership is an attitude.
- Leaders are visionaries.
- Leadership is about charisma.
- Leaders must be both tough and tender.
- Leaders are born.
- Leaders can be made.

Leadership, we're told, is the ability to do the right things, not just do things right (that's plain old *management*!). It's all about change, says former Harvard Business School professor John Kotter, while management is about dealing with complexity.[3]

Fons Trompenaars and Charles Hampden-Turner, two European experts on leadership, say that the big difference between managers and leaders is in their sleeping problems. Some managers can't sleep because they haven't met their objectives, while some leaders can't sleep because "their various objectives appear to be in conflict and they cannot reconcile them."[4]

In a famous *Harvard Business Review* article, Abraham Zaleznik writes, "Managers aim to shift balances of power towards solutions" while leaders "develop fresh approaches to long-standing problems and open issues to new options."[5]

And Warren Bennis and Burt Nanus, in their best-selling 1985 book *Leaders*, tell us that whereas managing means "to bring about, to accomplish, to have charge of or responsibility for, to conduct," leading is "influencing, guiding in direction, course, action, opinion."[6]

If you're confused already, just wait.

Depending on whom you listen to, you'll learn that leadership is a talent, a skill, a discipline, a process. The work of leaders is to see possibilities where others see only problems … to make strategic calls … to be decisive … to communicate compellingly … to negotiate skilfully … to win the support of stakeholders … to be comfortable with ambiguity … to motivate people. And a whole lot more.

Leaders are likely to be tall white males (in the West) … have advanced degrees … display emotional intelligence … be excellent networkers … have enormous physical energy … work hard and play hard … and – maybe most important of all – have balls.

Some gurus tell us leadership is like conducting an orchestra or herding cats. That it demands empathy, love, soul, and sensitivity. They borrow ideas from chaos theory and "the new science" and admire Robert K. Greenleaf's idea of "servant leadership."

Others say *blah*: real leadership is about winning, about beating the odds; that it takes toughness, a ruthless streak, a Machiavellian mind. They revel in war stories about "Neutron Jack" Welch, revered "Chainsaw" Al Dunlap as a man among men, think bellowing Steve Ballmer is a real hero, and see making the list of "toughest bosses" as the ultimate badge of honour.

While much of this may be true, it's hardly *useful*. What are you supposed to *do* with this information? If you're not a leader yet, how do you become one? If you are in charge already, how can you improve your performance? How do you tell if someone has the potential to be a leader? If you're trying to grow the next generation of leaders, where do you start?

Promises, promises

It's hard to imagine that a professor of surgery could earn his post without ever picking up a scalpel. No accounting teacher could qualify without being able to construct a profit and loss account or analyse a balance sheet. But *leadership* – why, that's different.

Most people posing as leadership gurus have led nothing themselves. In fact, they may not even have spent much time *near* a real leader. But hell, anything as interesting and important as this is an opportunity for instant wealth.

So you can pick up the ten keys to leadership success in under an hour from any number of books, magazines, audio tapes, videos, and websites. If that sounds like hard work, you can sit back and learn all you need to know from some shrieking motivational speaker (who's probably about 25 and has never had a proper job). For an afternoon of fun, you might try paintball games. Or if you think shock treatment is a good idea, you can hone your leadership skills in a white-water ride down the Zambezi River or bungee-jumping off the Victoria Falls bridge.

You can learn to be a leader – visionary, influential, powerful, globally respected, highly paid, etc. – from more people than could show you how to fly a kite. (Or if that doesn't grab you, and you'd rather teach than do, why not become a leadership coach yourself? *Anyone* can do it with the help of franchise operators who sell "the secrets" for less than you'd pay to set up a rubber stamp shop!)

If only it were that easy.

Many paths

Leadership is an elusive concept. I've been fascinated for many years by the difference between people at the head of organizations, and the rest. Who were these rare birds, and how did they get there? What got them noticed when they were among the Dilberts? What did they do along the way that gave them the edge over equally smart, aggressive, hungry, and maybe ruthless competitors? What lets them attract followers, persuade others to do their bidding, achieve great things, and earn fawning admiration – and fabulous sums of money?

And what about those others who, with little fuss or fanfare – and often without huge rewards – beaver away in their corners, making things happen, making a difference, and making the people around them special?

What turns leaders on? What gets them up in the morning and keeps them going during the day? Why are they more creative, more reliable, more persevering, and more effective than others? What can you learn from them that will help you spread the success virus?

Of course, there are as many answers to these questions as there are leaders. We are, after all, talking about a human ability and human traits. And we're talking about an activity that takes place in a complex, changing arena where small changes trigger big ones, and where a minor shift over here quickly becomes a major issue over there.

Leadership is not the product of a simple formula. Every age throws up a few "golden people" who seem to have arrived on the world stage at just the right moment. Some have spent years in preparation for their appearance. For others, it's a case of being in the right place at the right time. Always, a confluence of factors connects individuals to the possibilities for which they seem to have been born.

Jack Welch credits his mother with preparing him to be a leader. Disney chairman and CEO Michael Eisner thanks the head of his high school. Ricardo

Semler, author of the best-selling book *Maverick* and majority owner of Brazil-based Semco, says he learned most from Lewis Carroll, who wrote, "If you don't know where you're going, any road will take you there."[7]

Leaders come in every shape and size, from both genders, and from every race group, social class, and personality type. Some, like the legendary General George Patton, lead from the front. But then there are the "quiet leaders" like those singled out by Jim Collins in his *Good To Great* study, who combine humility and will to get their way.[8]

Leadership is part instinct, part skill. It's something you're born with and that you learn. It's an amalgam of logic and luck, power and compassion, teaching and learning, reflection and action.

There's no perfect way to identify or develop leaders. For every apparent answer there are more questions and contradictions. But there are also some clear lessons. By absorbing and applying them, most people can do better than they imagine, and probably gain all they wish for. They can make better decisions for themselves and their organizations, and make a real impact on those around them.

The first lesson is that leadership is only partly about you and largely about those around you. You have to look inward to have outward influence. You have to recognize that the power you get when you're anointed "Leader" is a one-time gift. To keep it, you have to keep earning it.

Great through others

Some people make a difference by excelling as solo performers – musicians, consultants, scientists, sportsmen and women, actors, and artists come to mind. They're a fine example to others, and have great influence. You can't over-estimate their value to society. But while it's one thing to seek *personal* satisfaction or success and glory, it's something else entirely *to be all you can be through others*. And that's what this book is about.

My definition of leadership is simple. It is:

The achievement of a specific purpose through others.

The key words there are *achievement* (results) ... *purpose* (for a reason) ... *through others* (by empowering and inspiring them).

This view makes three things clear:

1. It's not enough to merely have the title of chairman, CEO, vice-president, general manager, or whatever. You're accountable and you're measured by what you *do*, not what you *say*.
2. You need to be able to explain your intentions, and they must make enough sense for others to want to support them.
3. This is not a solo performance. What matters is your ability to unleash the potential in others, align their efforts, and keep them enthused over time.

There's a germ of leadership within almost every human being. There are leaders in many places in every organization. There's potential for even more of them. We lead people above us, below us, and beside us (Figure 1-2), and there's room to do it better.

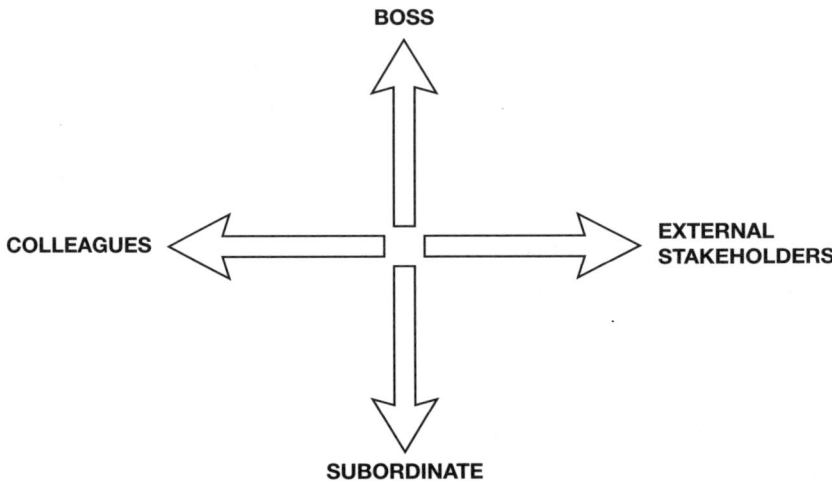

Figure I-2 *Four views*

If I can magnify your contribution by just one per cent, and if you, in turn, can magnify the next person's contribution by one per cent, the multiplier effect will be immense. Obstacles will melt away. Distant goals will be within reach. Unimaginable achievements will be possible.

The extended enterprise

Even in this "virtual" age, the edges of most organizations are quite clear. You can see where a company ends and the outside world begins – where "the rubber meets the road." But the line is blurring. Firms have to be not merely *mindful* of outsiders, but clear about the value, influence, risks, and threats inherent in being part of an extended "ecosystem." They have to understand what's needed to manage a widening array of players with many different agendas. And they have to be proactive and systematic in balancing those agendas.

If leadership is about getting results through others, you need to embrace all the "others" who can make a difference. In some cases, just one person counts. Most often, though, cooperation and collaboration with many individuals and organizations is essential. So *for real and enduring success, you need to create a "community of champions." The more superstars you have on your bench, the better.*

Some might be easy to find. Their names are up in lights, they're already acclaimed performers, and your only challenge is to sign them up. Others need to be carefully identified, trained, and nurtured.

Your ability to lead increasingly hinges on your ability to build and sustain relationships. Relationships, in turn, are a consequence of strategic conversation. Manage that well, and you can win stakeholder "votes." Manage it poorly, and you never have a chance.

The scorecard

Leadership is measured by hard facts and sometimes vague opinions. You need to be clear about what matters to you. But you also need to know what matters to others. Then, separate the "must do" factors from the ones with the most vocal advocates, and apply your resources where, on balance, they'll make the *best* difference.

Ask business leaders what their most critical goal is. Most will say, "To create value for our shareholders." This is hardly surprising, given the pressure they're under from analysts and investors. However, other stakeholders are now clamouring for attention.

Enlightened executives understand that while money is one measure of performance – and undoubtedly the most important one – it isn't the only one. Quarterly financials are a short-term yardstick. Annual reports give a more complete view. Over the long haul, many other factors come into play.

Assessing corporate performance has become a growth industry with many formulas. For example:

- There's a growing trend towards holding leaders accountable for a "triple bottom line" which balances economic profit with social and environmental responsibility.[9]
- Fans of the balanced scorecard use four key "perspectives": financial, customer, internal, and learning and growth.[10]
- According to a survey by PricewaterhouseCoopers, investment decisions are made on the basis of nine measures: earnings, cash flow, costs, capital expenditures, R&D investment, segment performance, strategic goals, new product development, and market share.[11]
- *Fortune* magazine's annual list of "Most Admired" US companies rates firms by another eight criteria*: innovation, financial soundness, employee talent, use of corporate assets, long-term investment value, social responsibility, quality of management, and quality of products and services.[12]

Fortune also reports on "the coolest companies to work for." There are numerous awards around the world for everything from product design to productivity, from safety to support for the arts. Every management function – customer service, personnel, IT, risk, assets, facilities, credit, energy – offers a chance to win a prize.

* The global list has a ninth attribute, "globalness."

With all this excitement, it's tempting to have a bash at everything. But that's a sure-fire way to end up with nothing. Organizations are the sum of their parts. While it makes sense to encourage leaders in every area to push their performance to the limits, you also have to keep them focused on the overarching goal and working as a team.

Performance is the result of a host of activities. You can measure it in many ways. But in the end, money talks. You have to produce more than you use. And you have to produce more every year, for you to have credibility and for your company to survive. Excellence in anything else is either a means to that end or an exercise in futility.

Leadership is a delicate balancing act. You can't satisfy everyone all the time. No decision is made in a vacuum. Virtually every move has its enemies.

Sometimes, you'll have the luxury of being able to make a call on the basis of hard facts. More often, you'll have less information than you like. Things will be unclear and ambiguous – and you'll need to be ambiguous in explaining your future moves.

Paradoxes will tear you this way and that. "Either-or" choices won't be an option. You'll have to slash jobs while motivating the survivors, think both global and local, give customers more for less, and so on. "This-and-that" will be the only way.

And always, you'll need to show sensitivity to public opinion – a vague target, if ever there was one. You'll need to inform, placate, correct, and win over the media, organized pressure groups, legislators, politicians, institutions, organizations, and innumerable individuals whom you may or may not know.

Leadership is a public relations job. You have to manage both your image and that of your firm, in a hostile world where opinions change with the wind. But as public relations experts know, hype has no chance against truth. If you're not utterly sure of who you are and what you must do, you'll have an uphill struggle. If you don't define your own sense of purpose, your personal values, and your character, it'll be done for you. And if you don't deliver what you've led others to expect, you shouldn't be surprised when they blow you away.

The measures you choose send powerful signals. They define expectations and focus the efforts of your organization. They also let you assess your progress and make course adjustments. So choose them with care and treat them with deadly seriousness. They'll make or break you.

The "X factor": followers

Leaders need followers. Your performance depends partly on you and mostly on them. What matters isn't your ability to take daring decisions or make stirring speeches, but rather that you get more from your team than anyone else could do.

Your followers may be either *conscripts* or *volunteers*. Conscripts have little choice but to be there. They desperately need the job, or can't easily move. Volunteers *want* to be there. They have other choices, but turn up because for them it's the best game in town.

Leaders of conscripts have an awful time. They have to drag people into the future. The only way they get things done is by using orders, threats, anger, arguments, and punishment. Their "followers" fear and resent them. Creativity is a rare thing in their firms – except to duck the system. People do only what's demanded of them. No one "goes the extra mile."

Leaders of volunteers, on the other hand, have it quite different. Their biggest problem is to harness the enthusiasm of their people, and align their energy.

There's no question that some people seem by nature to fit the conscript type, while you can't imagine others as anything but volunteers. But there's no arguing either, that leaders get the followers they deserve. Douglas McGregor was right when he wrote in 1960 that an executive's *expectations* shape the behaviour of the people they manage.[13] His insight of more than four decades ago has been proven too many times to ignore.

"Toxic" leaders expect the worst of people. They rely on "the system," "procedures," power, and other such weapons in their efforts to get things done. They frustrate themselves, because they foster a climate in which secrecy prevails and covering your ass is the first priority.

"Nourishing" leaders, in contrast, expect the best of people. Their tools of choice are dialogue, respect, trust, openness, challenges, and praise. They create a climate in which problems are opportunities and everyone's a hero.

The gift of winning

This book captures the essence of what leadership is about. It embraces ideas from many sources, and from my own experience of working with and observing many leaders.

Discovering the Essence of Leadership is based on this fact:

Only by being truly yourself – and true to yourself – will you enable others to be what they can be.

Leadership is a journey of discovery. It's both a journey in search of yourself and a journey in which you help others search for their essence and possibilities. Neither journey is ever complete. There are no limits to personal growth.

You discover your self partly through introspection and reflection, and mostly through experience. No matter how deep you dig into your mind, you only discover what you can do when you do it. Quiet contemplation has great value. But action provides the real test and the best learning.

In the same way, the performance and growth of the people you lead depends on their own thoughtfulness and action. As their leader, you can provoke both or inhibit them. Your choice will make or break them. And you too.

Leadership is a gift. It's a role you get partly because you have what it seems to take, and largely because others deem you worthy and give you the job. Consider this cycle of reciprocity:

1. You may decide that you want to be a leader, and you may prepare yourself carefully for such a role, but you need certain gifts in order to have a chance.
2. Usually, you must be chosen to lead. Someone else decides to give you the job. It's their gift to you.

3. You, in turn, have a gift for those you lead: the gift of discovering their potential.
4. They then have a gift for you: the gift of success as a leader.

This extraordinary relationship begins and ends with integrity. You have to face up to who you are. You have to reveal yourself as you are. And you have to live your own life. At the same time, you have to accept others as they are, and empower them to be whatever only they can be.

That is the essence of leadership.

The payoff

Being a leader has its perks, but it's not easy. If we remember few people as being great leaders, it's because the job is so onerous and the chances of failure are huge. If you wish to stick your neck out and be a leader, don't have any illusions about what lies ahead. On the public stage, you're fair game. Your own mistakes may not be your worst problem.

On the other hand, if you do have what it takes, if you have the guts to go for it, and if you can make a difference that matters, you'll have the satisfaction of knowing that you walked to the edge ... and flew.

1
THE PERSON

"It seems to me that at bottom each person is asking, 'Who am I really? How can I get in touch with this real self, underlying all my surface behaviour? How can I become myself?'"

Dr Carl Rogers, psychologist[14]

"What we need now is strong leadership."

"Where are the leaders who will get things done?"

"Without a leader, this lot will never win."

How often don't we hear these clichés? When a country faces a political problem, a city has to deal with a crisis, a company is in trouble, or a sports team hits a losing streak, these are the things people say. Somewhere, they think, there's *someone* who'll have the answers. Someone who'll sort out the mess, show the way forward, and get things back on track.

And when we speak of these rare birds, we say things like this:

"He's a born leader."

"She showed real leadership qualities."

"His remarkable leadership skill saved the day."

But what does all this mean? What exactly are we looking for? What do we expect from those we choose to lead? Is this about character, training, skill, or what? If it's about character, what traits should we look for? If it's about training or skill, what must we teach those who would be leaders?

Managers vs. leaders

Let's begin by agreeing what we're talking about. And a good place for that is the management vs. leadership debate.

Back in the dark ages of business theory, management involved planning, leading, organizing, and control. Then Philip Selznick, John Kotter, and many others decided this wasn't good enough. Leaders and managers, they said, are not one and the same. The first are change agents. The second are implementers. The functions are different, and require different people.

But this is just splitting hairs. Kotter, for one, contradicts himself when he writes, in his 1995 book *The New Rules*, "The number one *managerial* objective in most big firms should be creating a revolution"[15] (my italics). Willie Pietersen, a professor at Columbia University Business School, says that "the central challenge facing many managers today is to *create and lead an adaptive enterprise* – an organization with the built-in ability to sense and rapidly adjust to change on a continuous basis."[16] And according to Robert Eccles and Nitin Nohria of the Harvard Business School, "the purpose of management is fostering action and then making that action meaningful to people both collectively and individually."[17]

And leadership is ….

Surely, when you get down to the nitty-gritty, both managing and leading involve precisely the same thing:

The achievement of a specific purpose through others.

Now, what might that purpose be?

The first social responsibility of a business, as Peter Drucker points out, is to stay in business. So it has to make a profit. And to keep doing that, it must adjust to changing conditions in the world around it. Therefore, someone has to *make decisions*: which customers it will service, and how it will do so, which tasks to work at and which to abandon, how to relate to various stakeholders, how to get the necessary resources, and so on. And someone must *make things happen*: invent things, close sales, improve processes, collect debts, and much else besides.

Can one person both decide *and* do? Of course they can. And they should. It wasn't usual practice in the Industrial Age, and even today there's a sharp "division of labour" in many firms. But at a time when people are expected to bring their brains to work, when their knowledge, insights, and imagination are essential competitive weapons, it's the only way to go.

I'm not suggesting that everyone should have a bash at everything. What I am saying is that to be rigid and play only by the rules (on your organization chart) is foolish.

Sometimes, one person – Douglas, say – will be best suited to make a particular decision. He's in the right place at the right time, with some or all of the facts, and possibly the right experience under his belt. What's more, he might also be the one to turn the decision into action.

Under different circumstances, Beth might be thrust into the decision-making role. But she might do best by leaving implementation of her decisions to others.

There are no hard and fast rules about this. Once again, it's a matter of judgment. It comes down to *what feels best at that moment.*

In "normal" circumstances, leaders can go by the book. They can be nice to everyone and keep everyone happy. With the luxury of time, they can coach and mentor, consult and debate, lobby and delegate.

In a crisis, however, there might not be time to separate deciding and doing. When the shit hits the fan, the boss has to act fast. She not only has to make a snappy decision about what to do, but must also get it done. The best way might be to do it herself. If this upsets a few people, so be it. Saving a deal, soothing a customer, or keeping the company afloat is more important than trying to win a popularity contest. This is no time to be paralysed by theory. Whether the leader is "hands on" or "hands off" is of no consequence when there's work to do.

In all cases, though, the principle should be that *all* people are given the best shot at being great. That they are stretched, challenged, and tested. That they're treated like thinking, competent adults, not immature kids. And that they get the information, the support, and the resources they need to fly.

Clearly, there are different roles for leaders.

At one extreme, you might be the CEO of a major corporation. You're responsible for the growth of the business as a whole, and for everything that will deliver consistent long-term returns to shareholders. You have to think about the grand strategy, manage your board of directors, develop symbiotic relationships with a wide range of stakeholders, and much else besides.

At the other extreme, you could be head of the mailroom. Your mandate is narrower, and you have fewer "big" worries. But you still have work to oversee, and people to lead.

Somewhere between these jobs, you could be the branch manager in a small town. You have less to do than the CEO but more than the mailroom boss. Again, though, you're a leader.

Unleash the magic

It's hard to see what benefits there might be in continuing the management vs. leadership debate. As far as I can tell, its effects are mostly negative.

1. **It proceeds from the assumption that there's a neat black-or-white answer.** It kills any more subtle possibility. You're a leader *or* you're a manager, and that's that. So don't meddle in the other's territory. Don't modify your behaviour to suit changing conditions. Don't concern yourself with the hard work of implementation if your real job is to contemplate the big picture, and don't think about the big picture if you're a doer.

2. **Because it boxes the functions, it also boxes people.** Executives complain about "silos" in their organizations, then apply labels to ensure there are indeed silos. They plan "leadership" retreats at fancy resorts, and get Henry Kissinger or Robert Rubin to address them. "Managers" go to crummier places, and if they're lucky they're lectured by experts in quality or lean production. Organization charts, offices, dining arrangements, and cars all signal that no one really means "We're a team; we're all in this together." Any notion of equality is a non-starter.

3. **It offers an easy cop-out when things go wrong.** "We need leadership here" implies that the current team is perfectly able to perform, but has come

unstuck because of someone "higher up." They've been neutralized through no fault of their own, and will stay that way until someone not already in place comes to the rescue. (And of course, things grind to a halt while you search for a saviour.)

Of course, there's no arguing that some jobs require special insights or inspiration. Others are more mundane. Fixing a company in trouble isn't the same as keeping the books or producing another 10,000 widgets. Conquering new markets is a very different task than running a call centre or the quality lab. But all these jobs can be done brilliantly, quite well, or badly. The difference is what sends one company to the top of the pile and drives another into the dirt.

"Leaders" and "managers" are *labels*, not jobs and certainly not people. Banging on about the differences might give the gurus their thrills, but it does nothing to move a firm forward.

My advice is to ban the management vs. leadership debate from today. Stop harping on the differences. Stop the pointless conversation that demotivates people and kills their performance. Start talking instead about the possibility of unleashing the magic in all of them.

Born or made?

There have been many attempts to pin down physical or intellectual differences between leaders and the rest of us. Some studies suggest that *when* you're born is more important than *what* you're born with – that first-born children have the edge because they get more attention, have less competition early in life, try things first, take the lead in games, and are generally expected to set an example. Abraham Zaleznik argues instead that it's less important to be born first than to be *re*-born. "Once-born" individuals travel easily through life, he says; they fit well and develop personalities suited to maintaining order. Those who are "twice-born," on the other hand, struggle to find order in their lives; they have feelings of "profound separateness" and are driven to change things.[18]

The weight of evidence suggests that is that it's the totality of our natural endowments and our life experience that makes us what we are. That what ultimately matters is not how we *start* our lives, but how we *live* them, and that leadership is largely a learned skill.[19]

Ideally, leaders should exhibit some very specific traits: integrity, courage, incisiveness, decisiveness, perspective, and perseverance. They should also be skilled relationship-builders. And their track records should confirm all this. But often – and especially when you need to fast-track people – you have to take your chances and hope for the best.

So no recruitment or development programme should shut out people on the basis of how, when, where, or to whom they were born. No individual should be made to think, "I don't have what it takes because I didn't arrive with the right stuff." Selection processes must give people a fair chance. Organizations and their leaders must provide a context in which people will be more likely to succeed than fail.

Not all equal

Face facts. We are not born equal. We can't all be top of the class. But it really doesn't matter. There's magic in each of us.

Of course, *everyone* cannot manage *any* thing they might wish to. Even though we begin life with roughly the same number of cells, the same gene structure, and the same basic instincts, we won't all cross the same finish line and we definitely won't all cross it at the same time. To suggest that all of us have what it takes to be a Churchill or a Gandhi is pure fiction.

Getting to the top of almost any organization is hard work. Your own capabilities and efforts matter, but many other factors – including politics, patronage, and luck – play a part. Some people, apparently with all the right stuff, apply themselves diligently, do all the right things, and make a success of everything they do. Yet they lose out in the finals. Others are loyal soldiers who fight a good fight but win few medals. Then suddenly they're thrust into the general's seat – and become heroes.

You can ready yourself to stand out, and never do so. Or you can travel right to the end of your career before making your mark through circumstances not of your making. Some people dream of being leaders and never make it. Others dream of everything else, and are suddenly thrust into the limelight and rise to the occasion.

Fortunately, the right person often arrives just when they're needed. But many executives are meticulously prepared for The Big Job, then let us down when their moment comes. They're carefully headhunted, subjected to batteries of tests, vetted by experienced boards, and appointed with plenty of fanfare and support, only to quickly lose the plot.

Every year, US business schools graduate some 100,000 MBAs. Most get good job offers while they're still on campus. Most can expect to earn substantially more in their lifetimes than non-MBAs. Many will become chief executives, powerful politicians, or heads of hospitals, universities, or NGOs. Yet only a few will become stand-out champions.

It's the same in every other field.

I can ride a bike, but I'm not Lance Armstrong. Ernie Els is an exquisitely talented golfer, but he's not Tiger Woods. There's only one Margaret Thatcher, one Bill Gates, one Desmond Tutu, one Nadine Gordimer, and one Richard Branson. In every field, superstars are born, and the mould is broken.

Fortunately, though, every leader does not have to be a superstar. It takes all types to make a winning team. Many apparently ordinary people make important contributions to their companies, communities, and countries. They set records, win accolades and awards, make headlines, and "leave footprints in the sand." They may not be giants in the grand scheme of things, but the world wouldn't be the same without them.

We live in an age of hype and hero-worship, when celebrity status is the ultimate high. But it takes more than a handful of unusual individuals to make a country or a company great. That becomes possible only when you and I and many others realize our potential and decide to pursue our dreams with all we've got. When that happens, and when enough people make that decision, the earth moves. Soon, there's a critical mass of focused imagination and spirit, and remarkable things occur.

Out of the blue

Companies are "leadership factories." To survive and thrive, they have to put in place the processes, systems, and support mechanisms that will deliver talent for tomorrow. But they must also acknowledge these realities:

- **Leaders aren't always obvious before they become leaders.** People who by every criterion seem quite unremarkable one day can prove utterly outstanding the next. A lot of top executives pride themselves on their ability to "spot talent." But if that's true, why aren't more of their successors superstars? How is it that they overlook people who suddenly emerge as out-of-the-ordinary performers – too often at another firm? (And how come they promote so many duds?)

- **Leaders need a chance to lead.** Power and influence are critical assets, gained through promotions, mentorship, favouritism, or connections. But they only become apparent when the opportunity arises to use them. That might take a slump in business, a shift in the macro environment, new competitive threats, or some other "inflection point."

- **Leaders need things to go their way if they're to shine.** Sure, they must demonstrate over and over that they can meet trouble head on and win. They must be able to buck the odds. But they also need things to go their way. They need a customer to sign a big deal; a competitor to back down, make a dumb move, or go out of business; a regulator to pass a law that swings things in their favour; or their board to support them in a sticky situation. Whether by design or luck, leaders need some breaks.

- **Leaders come in every shape, size, and personality type, and from every kind of background.** Statistically, most US presidents are tall men. But does this mean the job can't go to a shorty? Or a woman? And what about evidence that leaders have fine presence, are blessed with both cognitive skills and emotional intelligence, are outgoing and gregarious types, great communicators, MBAs, low-handicap golfers, and so on? The simple answer: *it depends*. Sometimes yes, and sometimes no. This is about human beings, after all.

    Some may be born with what seems to be a head start: they have strong bodies, sharp minds, and wealthy, well-connected parents. They're given the best education, exposed to interesting people, encouraged to have confidence, and given every chance to excel. Maybe they show early promise. Maybe they perform well for many years. Yet when their moment comes, they cannot seize it. Or they're overlooked, because for any one of a million reasons, someone else gets the nod.

Others, seemingly less gifted, and with little or no help, become exceptional. Somewhere along the line something changes and they escape their ordinariness. They're in the right place at the right time … opportunity knocks … a door opens … they step into the sun.

These latecomers might be ambitious, and might have fought hard and long to get to the top. But the final leap to the boss's seat is a big one. There's only one Number One. You can make many decisions that will take you a long way through life, but this final promotion is in the hands of someone else. You don't decide to *get* it; they decide to *give* it.

Suddenly … Sir Rudy

Shortly after America was attacked on September 11, Jack Welch, former chairman of General Electric, and himself named by *Fortune* as "manager of the century," was asked who, in his view, was an outstanding leader. Without hesitation, he shot back, "Rudy Giuliani."

His reasons? When the World Trade Center was hit, the mayor of New York City got to the scene fast, ensured that emergency services were in place, and acted to calm not just his city, but the nation. (At that time, US president George W. Bush was still zigzagging across the country in Air Force One, under instructions from the Secret Service.)

In the days that followed, Giuliani stayed visible and signalled that he was firmly in charge. *Time* named him "Person of the Year" for 2001. In February 2002, Queen Elizabeth made him a Knight Commander of the Order of the British Empire. Soon there will be movies about him.

Giuliani wasn't always a hero. To be sure, he had cleaned up New York City. He had taken on the Mafia and done a great job fighting crime. But he wasn't loved by everyone. His career was marred by various controversies. There was a huge gap between who he was and who he was to become.

Two months after the terror attack, with the nation still stunned and grieving, American Airlines Flight 587 plunged into the New York suburb of Rockaway shortly after take-off, killing 265 people. Not surprisingly, the crash sparked fears of another terror strike.

For Giuliani, this tragedy was another chance to show that he had "the right stuff." He was on the scene within 30 minutes, and stayed to encourage rescuers and comfort citizens until late into the night. His steady hand, so evident in the earlier incident, made the difference that mattered.

Rudolph Giuliani brought his whole life – his training and experience, his political skill, his character – as well as the power of his office to these events. But these events made him whole. Without them, he would surely have handed over his job to Michael Bloomberg, and gone off quietly to the next phase of his career. Instead, he was transformed.

Through events not of his making, in a moment not of his choosing, he became a leader among leaders. Abraham Lincoln, Alfred Sloan, Nelson Mandela, Rudy Giuliani … who would argue with this list?

Give me a break!

The shelf life of leaders is getting shorter. Rapid churn is common not only in America, but also in Europe, and even in Japan.

- "Today," says Paddy Miller, a professor at IESE Business School in Barcelona, "a leader's tenure can be considered *finished* after 3 years."[20]
- A *Business Week* cover story in December 2000 noted that "Two-thirds of all major global companies have replaced their CEOs at least once since 1986."[21]
- *The Economist* reported that in February 2001, 119 CEOs left their jobs at large US companies – up 37 per cent from the same month a year earlier.[22]
- According to a cover story in *The Economist* of 4 May 2002, "Business leaders are being knocked off their pedestals faster than Communist heroes after the fall of the Berlin Wall."[23]

One reason is that the pressure for performance is growing. Activist shareholders want their rewards fast. Glitches like recession, political upheaval, product recalls, labour strikes, currency fluctuations, and hostile competition don't impress them. In this "no excuses" environment, it really is tough at the top.

The record shows that 90 per cent of new companies and products fail. Few firms survive for more than 30 years.[24] As Michael Schumacher said after winning the Monaco Grand Prix in 2001, "First, you have to finish."

But just staying alive isn't enough. Improving results gets harder every year. Say your company has revenues of $100 million this year, and you grow sales by $30 million. Next year, investors expect *another* 30 per cent increase – but from a base of $130 million. So the climb gets steeper and tougher.

Consider:

- According to *Fortune*, "The ultimate, pragmatic reason for not aiming at targets like 15% is the sheer difficulty – indubitable for companies of size – of growing that fast over an extended period … During a 40-year period, from 1960 to 2000, after-tax corporate profits grew at an annual rate of just over 8%."[25]
- In one of his famous letters to his shareholders, Warren Buffett, chairman of Berkshire Hathaway, writes: "I would wager you a very significant sum that fewer than 10 of the 200 most profitable companies in 2000 will attain 15% annual growth in earnings per share over the next 20 years."[26]

Yet, despite the facts, executives continue to make wild predictions about growth and earnings, putting themselves under the whip in the process.

At the same time, there are other stresses.

Globalization means punishing travel schedules. The trend towards empowering people means a wider span of control. Stakeholder pressures mean more communication – and more firefighting. Executives must keep up with the latest technology, contend with cross-cultural conflicts, and negotiate complex cross-border mergers and acquisitions. They must juggle their time to attend to customers, analysts, the media, and many others who can affect their business results. And somehow they must also fit in their families and friends.

The fact that executive turnover is high is not all bad. It can benefit leaders' careers and may be essential to the renewal of their companies. But it has a costly downside. Learning a new job takes time – maybe 18 months or more.[27]

Your potential

The good news is: *all of us have more potential than we know*. And the reality is that if we don't test our limits, we never learn what we might be.

Life leaches out the best in most of us and leaves the ordinary. Youthful dreams and ambitions are lost in the struggle to survive, to get through each day, to just "fit in." Without real effort, mediocrity sneaks up on us and blunts the edge of our desire.

Maybe you think you're already doing as much as you can. You've climbed the ladder and achieved a lot. "I work like a dog," you say, "and can't do any better or go any further." But is that true? Do you really know what you're capable of? Have you really tested yourself … pushed the limits … gone to the edge? Not likely.

In any event, this isn't just about hard work. The world is full of people who work desperately hard, yet manage only to eke out a living. Effort alone is no guarantee of success.

What matters, instead, is where and how you apply that effort. If your time and energy are focused merely on survival, you'll be lucky to survive. If, on the other hand, you aim higher and strive to make a difference, then better things are possible.

But why should this be important? Does *everyone* have to be extraordinary? Isn't OK performance enough to make you feel OK? In an era of terrible time pressures and endemic stress, isn't mediocrity quite a healthy thing? Is bust-a-gut ambition everything? Is super-achievement the ultimate goal? Wouldn't we be happier if each of us could set the bar as high as we liked, if we could amble instead of sprint, if we could fumble a few catches and not be counted out of the game?

The simple answer is: yes, of course average is alright. We're not all super-human, and we're not all turned on by the quest to be superstars. Some of us are content to be ordinary – in fact, quite *like* the feeling of being so-so. There's a place for all of us, even those who don't want to be boss.

But surely the better answer is that by nature, *human beings are achieving beings*.[28] We're genetically wired to adapt and develop in a hostile, changing world. All of us have extraordinary potential. And since we are uniquely gifted among animals, we shouldn't squander those gifts. We owe that to ourselves and to those around us.

For selfish reasons, we might seek achievement, wealth, power, and fame. That's perfectly OK. But because we're human, and able to do more than satisfy our own needs, we surely shouldn't duck a larger responsibility: *to make a difference*.

You don't "go it alone" in the animal kingdom. Everything that walks, flies, swims, slithers, or hops is part of some kind of organization – a herd, flock, family, clan, clutch, gaggle, pack, swarm, hive, or whatever. Bugs, barbets, and baboons all have sophisticated social systems. But none comes close to *Homo sapiens* in two respects: the way we design our world and the way we nurture each other.

- Our range of choices is virtually infinite. We can decide where to focus our energies, what to do next, and how to use our resources.
- Our thinking ability is, literally, mind-blowing. We can invent, make, improve, and change things like no other being.
- Our communication ability is remarkable. Language lets us capture history, make sense of facts, learn from others, explain ourselves, share best practices, and determine our fate.
- We're care-givers without peer. Not just in the sense of rearing our young and ensuring each other's mutual safety and well-being, but also in our ability to bring out the best in one another.

Who are you?

In any discussion about leadership, integrity is a word that's likely to come up. That's not surprising, given that every day brings news of dishonesty in high places. What is surprising is that the word is seldom used in terms of personal authenticity. Yet this is the essence of leadership.

You are what you are. Accept this, and you have a chance of becoming all you can be. Trust yourself, and others will trust you too. Deny yourself, and live a lie, and you will inevitably be exposed. But the damage you do to yourself is just one tragedy. Worse is what you deny others. By diminishing yourself, you diminish them too.

Look in the mirror. Who do you see?

- Is that person someone you know and like and are comfortable being?
- Are you confident in your own skin?
- Are you at ease with yourself – pleased to be you?
- How well do you know yourself?
- Do you really know your strengths and weaknesses? Do you acknowledge them?

Each of us is coded and conditioned to be unique. Designed from birth to be different, we grow to be unlike anyone else. Accepting this, and knowing what we – and we alone – bring to the party, is the first and possibly most important requirement for being an effective leader.

Authenticity is a rare trait in humans. There are powerful social pressures on us to be "like the rest." As we grow, we're encouraged to dress, speak, act, and even think like them.

In theory, branded goods set us apart and help us craft our own identity. In practice, they make us part of the gang. Watch a group of young men in a mall, for example. They're all dressed in much the same garb – high-top Nike shoes with flapping laces, baggy Levi jeans hanging so low off their hips that the crotch covers their knees, Gap T-shirts, Oakley sunglasses. Their hair is gelled the same way. Their gestures and their slang are identical.

Just as teenagers mimic each other, so too do adults. The media see to it, as does schooling, time at university, membership of exclusive clubs or political parties, and corporate culture.

Being yourself isn't easy. You really have to fight conformity, or it'll slip quietly over you. But it's important that you do fight it. Your value lies not in being exactly like the people around you, but in being different. In being exactly, uniquely *you*.

This is a lifelong struggle. And of course there's a balance. To be different just for the sake of it can make you a pain in the butt. You can spend so much time and effort making your *point* that you forget your *purpose*. The reason to have a clear sense of who you are and what makes you special is so that you can use your strengths to work with others.

Legend has it that when Michelangelo was asked how he had created his magnificent sculpture of David, he said, "I just chipped away everything that wasn't David." By chipping away at what's not you, you start to find your essence.

Ask yourself, "What about me is *not* me?"
- What beliefs are not really mine?
- What values do I espouse that are actually someone else's?
- What language have I copied?
- What behaviours aren't natural for me?

Now ask, "What *is* me?"
- What turns me on?
- What makes me laugh … and cry?
- What stirs my imagination, inspires me, angers me, hurts me?
- What is my proudest achievement?
- What would I like to do more of … and less of?
- How would I really like to spend the rest of my life?
- What have I learned in my life's journey that is of value to me and others now?
- What strengths have I developed from my successes – and my failures?

No one is perfect. All of us have screwed up. But whereas some people are forever crippled by their bad moves, others become wiser as a result of them. Reflecting on your weaknesses is a powerful learning experience. It helps you to fully understand yourself. But wallowing in what's "wrong" is deadly.

When you beat yourself up, you etch "hopeless" on your brain. You become convinced that redemption and change are out of the question. Negative words and images overpower any positive thoughts you might have, and dysfunctional behaviour follows.

You may be tempted to try to fix all your weaknesses, but you'll do much better by identifying your *strengths*, celebrating them, and building on them. The same applies to your organization: focus on its strengths, and many of its weaknesses will take care of themselves.

Footprints in the sand

When people die and notices appear about them in obituary columns, it's remarkable how few people choose to say anything. Most of their messages are trite. Surely there was more to a life than this? Or maybe not.

There's an old Arab saying, "The dogs bark, and the caravan passes." And so it is, apparently for most of us. We think we matter, we think others care, but then we go and ... we're gone.

Almost every motivational book asks, "What would you like written on your tombstone?" It's a good question. There's little space on the average tombstone. You have to be brief. Like a political consultant or an advertising copywriter, you have to capture the whole story in a few words.

- What will your whole story be?
- What would you say about yourself, knowing your innermost thoughts and your darkest secrets?
- How do you think others might see you – and how would you like them to see you?
- Will your children and grandchildren be proudest of you if they can say, "He produced fabulous shareholder value" or "She grew the company's market share by 324 per cent"? Or would it matter more to them to say, "He gave others the chance to be great" or "She let them discover their potential"?

Human beings are fallible and frail. We all make mistakes, bend under stress, and get hurt as we make our way through life. Everyone has demons and fears.

To become all you can be, you must own up to who you really are. You must understand what drives you.

Your legacy is shaped by what you do with every day of your life. It's up to you whether you use your time on earth well, or squander it. Some people know exactly what they must do. They're driven by a clear purpose. Others drift, or try many things.

Some people are directed from within. "I don't care what others think," they say. "I live life my own way." Others do nothing without first considering the impact of their actions or how they might appear.

No one can say who'll turn out best. There's no right way; there are no certainties.

Thinking about your legacy is a useful exercise because it forces you to take a long view and to put things in perspective. It takes you away from the here and now, and helps you imagine your future and pinpoint your priorities.

The danger of hubris

Bold dreams and supreme confidence are important in leaders. But they must be balanced by down-to-earth pragmatism and humility. Never lose sight of the need to take "baby steps" on your way to greatness. And never forget you're "just one of us." Your journey isn't over just because you think you've arrived.

In the great dotcom meltdown, the company that everyone watched as stock prices plunged was Cisco Systems. It was the bellwether of the tech industry and a leading indicator of wider business investment trends. Chairman John Chambers had starred in a *Fortune* cover story in June 2000. A headline beside his picture asked, "Is John Chambers the best CEO on earth?" What heady stuff! Then, in the blink of an eye, Cisco's stock price fell from a high of $86 to below $20, wiping out $430 billion in value – one of the biggest losses of shareholder wealth in history. Yet in an interview in mid-dive, Chambers told the *Financial Times*, "I very rarely fail in my leadership."[29]

Maybe not. But statements like this are a lightning rod for trouble.

Bernie Ebbers, the flamboyant founder and chairman of WorldCom, was widely admired for his vision and daring deals. In 19 years, he'd made the firm a giant in the telecommunications industry. The corporate website greeted visitors with a statement few would challenge: "Welcome to WorldCom – the pre-eminent global communications company for the digital generation."

In 1999, Ebbers ranked No. 26 in a *Time Digital* list of "people who changed everything." He told the magazine: "I believe God has a plan for people's lives, and I believe he had a plan for me … You'll see people who in the early days of WorldCom took their life savings and trusted this company with their money. And I have an awesome responsibility to those people to make sure that they're done right."[30]

The share price that year topped $60. Then it nosedived. By April 2002, WorldCom's market value was just 4 per cent of what it had been at its peak. It fell out of the Standard & Poor's 500, and Moody's Investor Services gave its $32 billion debt a "junk" rating. Ebbers was forced to resign, and a headline in the *Wall Street Journal* on 1 May announced: "Bernie bites the dust."[31] (Two months later, global stock markets shook and the firm literally imploded as news broke that it was involved in the biggest accounting fraud ever.)

Another icon who fell from grace was Percy Barnevik. As CEO of ABB, he made it one of the most talked about companies in the world. His performance earned him the title "Europe's Jack Welch." After retiring from that job, he became chairman of Investor, the Swedish holding company that controlled ABB plus many other big firms. He was an outspoken advocate of good corporate governance, and given his stature, people took him seriously. But in 2001, news leaked that he'd awarded massive pensions to himself and his successor at ABB, Goren Lindahl, without board approval. That error of judgment cost him his reputation. Lindahl lost face too, as he was about to become chairman of Anglo American, and had to stand aside.*

Then there was Jac Nasser. He spent his whole working life with Ford, but only survived as CEO from January 1999 to mid-2001. By any standards, he

* Both men agreed to pay back half of their pensions.

introduced some visionary ideas to the company. He promised to give every employee a computer to bring them up to speed for the information age. He promoted the idea of teaching as a leadership tool. He sought to shift the company away from auto manufacturing and into the knowledge end of the value chain. He bought other famous car brands (Volvo, Jaguar, Land Rover). And he drove Ford into new ventures like e-commerce, aftermarket fitment, and even scrap metal recycling.

But despite his efforts, profits plunged. Differences between Nasser and chairman Bill Ford poisoned morale and got in the way of strategy. When the company was hit by a massive recall of Firestone tyres fitted to its Explorer, things came to a head. Nasser was forced out.

Obviously, a number of factors contributed to his fall. But those most cited were his penchant for flashy living, his imperious manner, and his relationships with the people whose support he needed. A company joke had it that while Jack Welch had ten people who would take a bullet *for* him, Nasser had ten people keen to put a bullet *in* him.[32]

Around the time that Nasser was going down, several other executives were reaching new heights. Ken Lay, Houston's favourite son, was soon to return to the top job at Enron (to the great relief of investors). Joseph Berardino was about to be elected, by an overwhelming majority of votes, as managing partner and chairman of Arthur Andersen. And the great Jack Welch, named "Manager of the Century" by *Fortune*, was about to retire as chairman and CEO of General Electric, launch a best-selling management book, and start a worldwide speaking tour that would draw huge crowds of awestruck executives.

The Enron scandal took care of Lay and Berardino – and tens of thousands of their hapless colleagues. Welch hurt his reputation – and that of General Electric – by having an affair with the editor of the *Harvard Business Review*. (She lost her job; the prestigious journal took a drubbing in the press; Welch's wife divorced him.)

When we turned into the New Century, corporate chieftains were the heroes of the age. They featured in lengthy profiles in business journals, were regularly interviewed on TV, made guest appearances on the Jay Leno show, and dined at the White House. Their annual trek to the World Economic Forum meeting in

Davos made that event a must for politicians, the heads of NGOs, Nobel Prize laureates, pop stars with a cause, and, naturally, the media. For all the fuss about their pay and their perks, and for all the flack they drew over globalization, business leaders were the centre of attraction.

That was then, and this is now.

By flying too close to the sun, many exceptional executives have burned their reputations in the past few years. In some cases, you could see trouble coming. In others, a gradual accumulation of small events added up to catastrophe. Often, one bad decision was all it took.

"The fashion for flamboyance in chief executives is definitely over," says *The Economist*, "at least until the next boom arrives."[33] That's possible while economies remain depressed, and given the war against terrorism, the rage against excess, and so on. But don't bet on this being a lasting trend. Human nature makes people ambitious, greedy, and flashy. Business offers them plenty of chances to reveal their weaknesses.

Success should never be taken for granted. Greatness is not to be treated lightly. As a leader, you have serious responsibilities. You're custodian of your own reputation and that of your company. You hold in your hands the well-being of employees, suppliers, investors, and the community at large. It's a perilous job, because the chances of success aren't good, and the forces against you are great.

Keep your feet on the ground

As a young executive, things change the minute you're identified as a "hi-pot."* Your colleagues become polite and helpful, even if they're envious, because they want to travel in your slipstream. People start filtering what they tell you, holding back information that may upset you and keeping you happy with mostly good news. As you rise to the top, there are more than enough butt-kissers to keep you convinced of your superiority, and cut off from reality.

* Having "high potential."

And when you get The Big Job, you also get the barriers of middle managers, assistants, and secretaries; the supplicant journalists (whose editors are mindful of your advertising clout); the compliant staff; and the hopeful beggars from charities, orchestras, art galleries, and zoos.

It's hard to keep your feet on the ground when everyone around you is so humbled, so interested, so admiring, so obedient, and so grateful in your presence. Self-importance is an occupational hazard.

But precisely because leadership is so heady and exciting, it demands extreme level-headedness. You need to remind yourself constantly that you hold your job at the pleasure of others, and that your role is to get things done through others. You need them more than they need you. Playing God won't win their votes. You may seem to get away with being imperious, and you may think people admire you for being curt and unreasonable, but these traits mark you. When you make a mistake, they come back to haunt you.

There are many ways to live your life. Leaders come in every stripe. Some are "wonderful human beings," polite, kind, and compassionate to the extreme. Others are awful to be around. Men and women in both categories achieve great things.

There's no point in arguing that one kind of behaviour guarantees results while the other brings failure. But unless you get pleasure in being disliked, what's the point in shoving your "greatness" down other people's throats? And if you need the help and support of people who have their own take on life, and their own needs, ambitions, and feelings, what's to be gained by abusing them?

Remember the golden rule

You can make things happen in many ways. You can speak softly or loudly, coax and cajole, or wield a big stick. Sometimes blowing your top works, and insults or threats do the trick. Other times call for a silver tongue, gentle persuasion, pure reason. There's no one best way. Circumstances dictate what's right.

But remember this: *good manners matter*. And since you're probably in this for the long haul, making people hate or fear you is not a good idea.

Resentful conscripts will never do as much for your cause as willing volunteers. Better to have the people behind you push you to great heights than off the edge of a cliff. Better to have them speak well of you when you're not around, than spread the dirt. And the only way to do that is to treat them with respect, and always to be civil.

"Do unto others as you would have them do unto you."

Many leaders demand respect. But you can't *command* it. If you don't give it, you won't get it. Making people grovel isn't the same as winning their admiration and support.

If the leaders of many organizations knew what their people said about them, they'd be horrified. Some might shrug and say, "Well, I'm not here to be Mr Nice Guy. I've got a job to do." Others might say, "Screw them. If they performed, I wouldn't have to be tough on them." These are feeble and foolish responses.

On many occasions, I've watched leaders of major companies treat their people in the most appalling way. Foul language and personal insults fly. Wild assumptions and selective facts reduce sensible discussion to sheer stupidity. Debate dies. A sullen silence settles. The boss has won.

They think.

2

The Work of Leaders aders

THE WORK OF LEADERS

"The artfulness with which you communicate – ironically enough, something you cannot measure – is becoming the most practical tool in the businessman's kit."

Bill Bernbach, co-founder Doyle Dane Bernbach[34]

So, leaders get results through others. Their challenge is to create "a community of champions" – who make each other great in their pursuit of collective greatness.

Leadership embraces seven essential tasks:

1. **Define direction.** In a world of opportunities, it's tempting to chase after too many of them. But "spray and pray" strategies don't work. Companies have to lay bets. They have to decide which opportunities are most promising for them (not just for *anyone*) – and which to walk away from.

   The leader of an organization doesn't have to be its chief strategist. But she does have to see that there is a strategy, and that everyone knows where to aim. She also has to keep them focused, and stop them straying every time something new and interesting appears on the radar screen.

   Setting direction isn't a one-time effort. As circumstances change, so must an organization flex and adapt. Sometimes the shifts are subtle – a few degrees this way or that will do. But often they have to be radical, in which case selling them is harder work.

2. **Decide priorities.** Most people make themselves ineffective by letting their "to do" lists get too long. They're loath to abandon anything. They know they'll never get around to every item on their lists, but keep them there all the same.

   Deciding what to do is quite easy – "everything" calls for attention. Deciding what *not* to do is much harder. So leaders must prune ruthlessly. They have to keep asking, "Will doing this get us closer to our goals, or take us further away?" Anything that doesn't make the right kind of difference must be taken off the list. Taking the easy way out – "Let's just keep Project X on the back burner" … "We can't afford to let any of our customers go" – is the kiss of death.

This is often easier said than done. When you're hustling for business, every customer seems critical. People with pet projects don't readily give them up. It's not always clear what the payoff from a particular activity might be. But remember the famous Pareto principle – the 80/20 rule. Test everything by the question, "Is this one of the 20 per cent of things that will give us 80 per cent of what we want?"

3. **Acquire, develop, and align resources.** Good intentions never become anything else if you don't have what you need to make them reality. And every organization has more possibilities than resources.

   The vision and mission statements of most firms are pure fantasy. They talk of futures that'll never happen. Their proud authors overlook the need for people, money, technology, and whatever else they need to turn their dreams into sales and profits.

   Without basic building blocks, no organization will gain traction in the marketplace or last for long. So leaders must build the infrastructure that'll take them to the future.

   Some resources must be bought. Some can be home-grown. All must be right for the task at hand, and must be aimed in the same direction. This is ongoing work. And since change is inevitable, constant realignment is essential.

4. **Inspire innovation.** Because there's so much information about, strategies converge at light speed. Companies race each other into a commodity trap. Today's breakthrough products and services are cloned overnight and quickly become ordinary. The business model that gives you an advantage one day is hopeless the next.

   Innovation can't be turned on and off at a whim. It has to be a way of life. You have to create an environment in which people constantly challenge convention, strive to make a difference, and define new realities, or you'll struggle forever to break away from the competitive pack.

The big challenge is to manage today's business soundly, while at the same time inventing *tomorrow's* business. This is not an either-or choice. Your current capabilities and customers fund your future; but if you don't pursue new ones, you won't have a future.

Balancing execution and innovation is a challenge at any time. It's especially hard in times of great change, or when your organization is being buffeted by external surprises.

5. **Drive action.** Inertia is easy – much easier than movement. So it's a state that most living things are comfortable with. Organizations are particularly prone to slowing down and grinding to a halt. If the people in them aren't constantly goaded into action and pushed for results, inactivity soon overcomes them. They may try to look busy for a while, but seldom keep it up.

Companies are especially vulnerable when they're *successful*. This is when they suffer a "hardening of the attitudes." Managers think they've cracked the secrets of success, and that "more of the same" will do. Systems become entrenched. No one questions processes. It's easier to repeat what worked yesterday than to go through the trauma of trying to do something new. "Different" and "better" become signals to batten down the hatches and justify doing nothing.

6. **Foster learning.** To survive in a hostile world, organizations must adapt and learn. Literally everything they do holds the promise of new insights.

Starting early in the 1990s, the idea of "learning organizations" took hold everywhere. I don't recall being at a strategy meeting in recent years where this hasn't been a goal. Yet most companies are far from making it reality. If anyone in them knows anything new, they keep it secret. Information and ideas are seldom shared. No one can say with certainty, "This is what we learned in the past three or four years. This is why it makes us better off. Here's how we're building on that knowledge."

Effective leaders know that tomorrow's stars may well be today's ho-hum performers, but with different stuff in their heads. So they create an environment where learning is a deliberate process, and where reflection is a key activity.

7. **Build confidence.** Fear of failure is crippling. Abraham Maslow warned against the "Jonah complex," which he called a "defense against growth." Human beings, he said, "are generally afraid to become that which we can glimpse in our most perfect moments, under the most perfect conditions, under conditions of greatest courage. We enjoy and even thrill to the godlike possibilities we see in ourselves in such peak moments. And yet we simultaneously shiver with weakness, awe, and fear before these very same possibilities."[35]

James Waldroop and Timothy Butler, directors of career development at the Harvard Business School, warn against "career *acrophobia*" – the fear of falling from great heights in one's career.[36] It's a common problem that causes people to shy away from challenges. (If trying something and succeeding will set you up for a fall, why do it?)

Some people arrive at work with enormous confidence. In their formative years, they've been convinced that they're wonderful and worthy. They'll tackle any challenge and won't hesitate to make their views known. But others – perhaps the majority – have a different sense of self. They're uncertain, hesitant, and cautious about sticking their necks out. When they argue, it's to cover their weaknesses rather than share their convictions and learn from people who see things differently. When they come up against a strong point of view, they get angry and defensive, or back down and sulk.

Confidence is a powerful competitive advantage. You can't see it, you can't measure it, and you can't easily instil it in people. But leaders must foster it, or they'll have to make every big decision – and many small ones – themselves.

There are dozens of complex theories about how you might do these things. But if a vital strength of leaders is their ability to separate wheat from chaff and to get right to the guts of a matter, let's do that right now.

What followers expect

It's time leaders faced this fact: what followers expect from you is that you *act like a leader*. That you:

1. Give them hope of a better future.
2. Give them a sense that you know what the hell you're doing.
3. Give them direction.
4. Give them opportunities to learn and grow.

No one expects you to know precisely what tomorrow holds. Nor do they expect you to know exactly how to deal with all of life's challenges. But they do want to know that you have a strategy, that it has a fair chance of working, and that marching along with you won't take them straight over a cliff.

"When I was a boy," writes Dr Laurence J. Peter in *The Peter Principle*, "I was taught that the men upstairs knew what they were doing."[37] Every society teaches reverence for those at the top. We're told to respect our leaders, bow to their superior knowledge, and follow their example. Yet time and again, they let us down. For all their bluster, it's apparent that they have no idea what they're about. They guess, improvise, play it by ear, and hope for the best.

To hold the attention of your followers and keep their confidence, you have to demonstrate that you know what you're about. Making fine speeches won't fool anyone for long. Nor will puffery in your company magazine do the trick. Either you prove your worth or you lose your clout.

Two frames

A firm's performance is determined by many things. Two of them stand out:
1. How its people perceive things (their world view).
2. How they feel in the workplace (the climate).

If these things don't get enough attention, nothing else matters. It won't help you to dive into six sigma quality, CRM, or team-based learning initiatives if you ignore these realities. Only by putting them at the top of your agenda will you have a chance of making the sophisticated stuff work.

Think of these as frames – as in picture frames. The first (Figure 2-1) contains your world view (your paradigms or "mental models"). It defines your strategies.

The second (Figure 2-2) defines the space in which people work – their operating context.

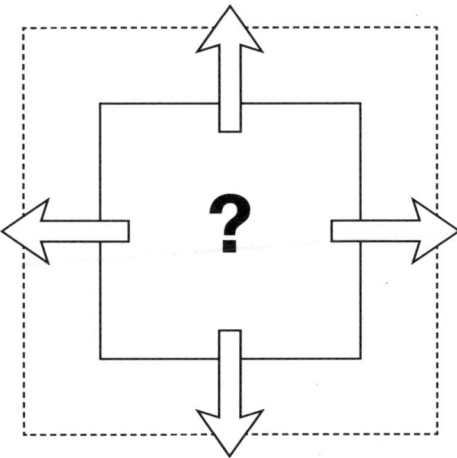

Figure 2-1: *The world view*

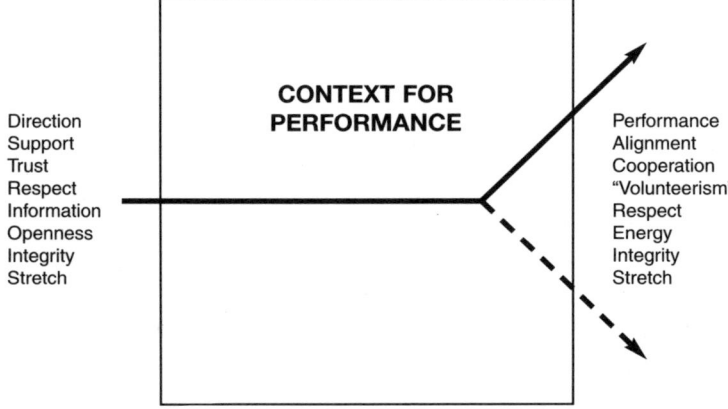

Direction
Support
Trust
Respect
Information
Openness
Integrity
Stretch

CONTEXT FOR PERFORMANCE

Performance
Alignment
Cooperation
"Volunteerism"
Respect
Energy
Integrity
Stretch

Figure 2-2: *The performance arena*

Every strategy is based on a particular view of the world. What we see is what we think about and what we respond to. It also affects *how* we respond. Some information is deemed important, so it's included. Much more is shut out. What's in the frame gets attention. The rest is downplayed or ignored.

In *Making Sense of Strategy*, I stressed the importance of strategic conversation – the dialogue and messages that focus resources, effort, and action. As I pointed out, the cliché that "what gets measured gets managed" is true, but it's only what gets *talked* about that will be either measured or managed.[38] And what's in the frame gets talked about.

- If you frame your *industry* as "building construction," that's where your mind will focus. You'll be interested in customers and competitors within that industry, regulations that govern it, and the technologies you need to operate in it. News about the fast food business, auto assembly, or paper manufacturing won't grab you (unless firms in those sectors want new buildings).
- If you frame your target *geographic market* as "Asia," that's where your team will concentrate. Their "antennae" will pick up the slightest hint of anything going on in that region. They'll unconsciously filter out every other place on the map. Events and opportunities in Europe, America, or South Africa will at best be of passing interest.
- If you frame "disk drives," "alloys," or "adhesives" as your *technological competence*, you'll be amazed at how information on these subjects leaps from a page of text, or from your computer screen when you surf the Internet. On the other hand, while you may read about gene splicing in *Time* or *Nature*, it won't ring bells. It'll be interesting, but not important. In each case, your subconscious will sort the good stuff from the rest.

Leaders also frame *issues* in ways of their choosing. "This law is bad for us," they say, "and if we don't get it changed we're out of business." So influencing regulators gets to the top of their agenda. Or they say, "Our first priority is to get costs out of our supply chain." So they become obsessed about outsourcing and alliances.

One leader talks incessantly about developing people. Another is fanatical about customer service. A third bangs on about technology. By their words, they direct their people. The way they see and explain the world becomes the way others see and understand it. Their priorities become everyone's priorities.

What you see and say

The results you get hinge partly on your use of information; your *attitude* may matter even more. Astute thinking is an advantage only when it's underpinned by a "can do" mindset. There's enough bad news in the media to paralyse anyone. But leaders can't let it get to them. They also have to deal with its effects on others. They have to move things forward.

Perceptions are reality. What you see in your mind shapes your beliefs and actions.

If you believe the latest economic signs are good for business, you'll feel bullish and act as if better sales and profits are in the bag. If you imagine a customer to be a tough SOB, you'll call on him with trepidation (and probably get screwed for a lower price).

Almost any factor in your environment – the HIV/AIDS pandemic, a new technology, changes in competition law, a tariff hike, or a strike at a supplier's plant – can be "good" or "bad" for you and your business, depending on how you see it and speak about it. As a leader, you have to be mindful that your world view colours your own actions, and that what you see and communicate to others has a profound effect on them. To see "the glass half full" rather than "half empty," to speak of "challenges" and "possibilities" rather than "problems" and "impossibilities," does more than put a positive gloss on a negative picture. *The words you choose impact directly on the results you get.*

Positive leaders inspire very different performance than negative ones.[39] Positive ones accept that everything will never go entirely their way. They know that in life, ups and downs are normal. They accept that setbacks are inevitable, and treat them as learning opportunities. When things go wrong, they quickly acknowledge the fact. Then they move on, better for the experience.

People who work for positive leaders know that being the bearer of bad news isn't the kiss of death. They know it's safe to "tell it like it is." They also know that when they do report trouble, they should have some ideas about how to deal with it. "We're stuffed" is not an acceptable opinion.

One executive I knew had a simple response to just about every problem. He'd listen patiently to the details. If there was a solution, he'd let the discussion run. If there wasn't, he'd say, "Next," and move on. There was no backtracking. He knew there was no point looking back and whining, "If only ...." He refused to get into post-mortems. And of course, his attitude was catching. At first people joked about it, but they soon came to see the wisdom in following his example.

Negative leaders latch on to any hint that their plans might be derailed. They're hesitant because "things might go wrong." They never have enough information. They second-guess every decision and see the slightest glitch as the end of the world. Instead of educating their people to look ahead, think about the great things they could do, and be purposeful and brave, they train them to look back over their shoulders, and to be unsure and timid.

Few leaders have any idea how much power they have to fundamentally change people's minds. Most are careless about what they say. They fail to see that their strategic conversation changes the way people think.

Get real

Positive thinking is a flaky subject. Its cheerleaders have earned a bad name for both the subject and themselves. Too many books and too many motivational speakers offer glib advice on how to shrug off lousy feelings and bring on good ones. Not for them the real and awful consequences of a depressed economy, a lost job, a family tragedy, or serious illness. And not for them the hard slog of recovering from these setbacks. Instead, they promise that if you adopt a precise number of "principles" or obey an equally precise number of "immutable laws," all will be well. Your greatness will pop forth and everything you want will be yours.

This clearly is nonsense.

Positive thinking isn't something to be switched on and off. You'll seldom get away with moping in your office but presenting a "happy face" to your team. Your real feelings will come out. People are extremely sensitive to their leaders' moods, and they're not fools. They might not know you've just got a hostile bid for your company or a nasty letter from the bank, but they certainly do know when the economy is on the skids and people are being fired everywhere.

Maintaining an upbeat mood doesn't require that you deny things are bad. It does require that you:

1. Look reality straight in the eye.
2. Get the facts on the table.
3. Acknowledge what's before you.
4. Concentrate on what you *can* do, rather than on what you *can't* do.

It's pointless doing this only when you hit trouble. Being reactive makes you vulnerable. Instead, you should prepare your organization for whatever lies ahead. The starting point is to make it "information rich."

A practical way to do this is by involving your people in scanning the environment, and discussing what it means to your company. Rope in as many of them as you can. Make it an ongoing process. Here are the benefits:

1. You get lots of eyes and ears and minds working for you.
2. Your team starts developing a shared sense of reality.
3. People learn that uncertainty and change are normal, and that confronting the truth is the smart thing to do.

Even if you can't be positive about the challenges you face, you *can* be positive about how you'll handle them. And you can keep your people focused on those actions rather than fretting about how terrible things are. The way to do this is:

1. Foster a strategic conversation that fixes on the *future* rather than the past.
2. Encourage people to define issues clearly.
3. Emphasize possibilities rather than impossibilities.
4. Develop multiple solutions.
5. Act to learn what works and to generate more options.

Many organizations spend fortunes trying to make people positive. Yet they unwittingly train them to be negative. They send downbeat messages through everything they do.

Optimism is a trait of too few people to be taken for granted. "Learned optimism" is a competitive strength you can build in yourself and in your team. Work on it, and you'll see a noted difference in what people say, in what they put on meeting agendas, in how they report on progress, and in the way they work together. In no time at all, they'll discover that they have it within them to fix things, deal with change, survive attack, and even cope with pain.

Organizational spirit is a key factor in competitiveness. You either ignite it or kill it by your words and deeds as leader. Leave it to chance, and you'll forever be in firefighting mode. Problems will always outnumber opportunities, and many will be insurmountable. But see spirit as a weapon of business war, and manage it carefully, and the sky is the limit.

Facts and assumptions

It's too easy, on the basis of "hard facts," to fool yourself. This market is easy to crack. That competitor is unbeatable. A colleague is lazy, stupid, not up to much.

But beware of jumping to conclusions. Being decisive is important, but to make up your mind without first surfacing your assumptions and testing them is the height of idiocy. Yet it happens all the time.

Assumptions are the foundations of people's beliefs, and thus underpin their decisions. Some may be based on relevant facts. Too many are grounded in un-connected information, rumour, hearsay, and experience – or even just *guesswork*. But they're cloaked in the guise of truth, so they get accepted without question.

There's a good deal of pressure in society to gloss over bad news and pretend that everything is wonderful. Economists have a terrible track record when it comes to their forecasts. They tend to be bullish rather than risk being accused of "gloom and doom" predictions. Executives, too, tend to err towards the upside. Very seldom do they predict a slump in sales or profits. After all, that's not what their shareholders want to hear, and it demotivates their people.

I've sat in countless management meetings where top executives have talked about the outlook, and I've marvelled at how they get away with utter bullshit. Over coffee before the conference, everyone complains how tough things are and why there's no relief in sight. Yet once the doors close and they get down to business, everything changes. The lines on their charts go up or down just the way everyone wants them to. The numbers are always better than last year's. Their markets are going to grow, their sales will sizzle, their future margins and profits are the stuff of dreams.

Setting stretch goals can inspire exceptional performance. But there's a fine line between doing that with full knowledge of the necessary facts, and believing in the Tooth Fairy. Leaders owe it to themselves and those around them to be as sure as they can of their ground.

One effective way to test assumptions is to apply that favourite tool of Japanese managers, the "Five Whys." Just keep asking "Why?" of every assertion, and keep digging till you hit bedrock. This helps separate fact from fiction and exposes the logic – or lack of it – in what people say.

Ideally, your probing should lead to truth and certainty. Sometimes it'll leave you with more questions than answers. However, if this raises the odds only slightly in your favour, then it's worth the effort (and the irritation it might cause in your team). Besides, it teaches your colleagues to:

1. Think through their assumptions and make them clear.
2. Back opinions with facts.
3. Make a sound case for what they're selling.
4. Explain themselves logically.

With practice, you'll become more incisive in your questioning. Your team will become more thorough about their homework, more alert to issues and trends, and less inclined to shoot from the hip.

Basics and breakthroughs

One of the greatest challenges to any leader is the need to balance stability and change, a focus on the *basics* with a drive for *innovation*.

The first principle of business competition is, "If you don't make a difference, you don't matter." You have to pick your "difference" with care, and stick with it. Chopping and changing is a recipe for disaster. You not only confuse your organization, you also confuse customers.

Every company needs to define its specific target market, craft a unique value proposition, and create an effective business model. Commitment to each of these is critical.

Except in a crisis, the first task of any leader is to *make the current business work*. If that doesn't happen, there's probably no way to fund the future, and you run the risk of creating something new on shaky foundations. The second task is to reinvent the business. To get these activities back to front is to court failure.

These questions focus attention on the priorities :

1. What are the basics that drive this business?
2. Does everyone know what they are and why they matter?
3. What are the consequences of ignoring them or starving them of resources?
4. How well do we do them right now?
5. What improvements or changes must we make?
6. If we do nothing new, what will the consequences be?
7. If we really need to make radical changes, how will we manage that process?

However, there's no escaping the need for innovation. Products and processes must be continuously improved. New offerings and new ways of delivering them must be invented. Every employee must be encouraged to "find a better way, every day."

Incremental change is relatively painless. Sometimes, you can get away with it for a long time. But sooner or later, radical change becomes necessary. That's far more difficult, and also potentially *dangerous* to an organization. For too much change, too fast, can tear a company apart.

Innovation can be provoked in many ways. You can set up "skunk works,"* offer incentives for new ideas, create forums for brainstorming, and so on. In practice, though, this doesn't always work as well as expected. Ideas come in bursts rather than as a flow. They come from few people rather than from many.

Ideally, innovation should be bred into your firm's DNA. Everyone can make a difference, and they should want to do it all the time. There's only one way to make this happen: ask every person in your company, every time you see them, "What have you done differently and better today?" Do this often enough, and they'll get the message and surprise you with their creativity. Skip it, and they'll keep doing more of what they were doing yesterday.

Innovation is a very sexy subject. It should be high on your agenda. But never forget what pays for it. Never let any of your people forget the basics. If you can walk this tightrope, anything is possible.

Building "strategic IQ"

Many people contribute to the performance of any organization. Some work near the CEO and get maximum guidance and support. Many more are out of sight, and out of mind too. In theory, they get their direction and instructions "through the channels." In practice, most of the information that influences them arrives informally and by accident, through the grapevine. Scraps of vital stuff – plus a good deal of gossip, rumour, innuendo, and even scandal – shape their beliefs and their attitudes, define their priorities, and influence their values.

Listen to leaders talk about *themselves*. They give the impression that they know exactly what's going on across their organizations, and are firmly in control. Few of them realize just how little they know and how *out of control* they are. Fewer still do what they might to improve their understanding of things at their organization's edges, and to manage their influence.

If you accept that you can't know or control everything, you have to ask: "So how can I be effective? How can I get the things done that I believe are important?

* Small teams dedicated to producing breakthrough ideas.

How can I ensure that people will do roughly the right things more often than they'll make costly mistakes?"

There is, of course, only one answer:

You have to equip them to succeed, then set them free.

Few things in life are guaranteed. One thing that's definitely *not* guaranteed is people's behaviour. No matter how much you train them and communicate with them, and no matter how much care and respect you show them, you can't be sure how they'll respond. Some will surprise you on the upside. Some will let you down. Yesterday's disappointments become today's heroes. Those you have every reason to believe in become tomorrow's failures.

Leaders have to accept these realities. Two strategies help you deal with them:

1. Raise the "strategic IQ" of your organization to give everyone the best possible shot at excellence.
2. Implement an "operating system"[40] that keeps the whole team "in the loop" and ensures rapid and regular feedback on issues and events that can affect the organization.

The strategic IQ of your organization reflects the ability of people individually and collectively to make sensible choices. It's a simple idea with weighty implications.

From my observations, too many organizations have a very low strategic IQ. Few of their people know what's important, what's going on, or what to do about it. Here and there, you may find pockets of "smartness." Overall, people are flying blind. They're mired in uncertainty, so they either do nothing or the wrong things. Their efforts are misdirected and waste is endemic. Many of the practices intended to enhance their effectiveness in fact cripple them.

The strategic IQ of any organization is a direct consequence of its strategic conversation. If the conversation is open and honest, information-rich and robust, it's likely to give people what they need to realize their potential. If it's lacking in these areas, they'll never perform. They might try hard to fight the system, to find out what they need to know through the back channels, and to motivate themselves. But their efforts will mostly be in vain. There's a point at which even the most extraordinary people are diminished by the companies they work in. Their spirit simply can't survive that critical mass of negative energy.

There might have been a time when strategic IQ was not terribly important. Some people would argue that even today it matters only in "knowledge organizations." They'd say that making everyone supremely smart in, say, a manufacturing firm, is just a recipe for frustration. But who can argue that informed people are the likeliest to produce quality products or propose new ways of cutting waste? And who can deny the *motivating effect* of information?

There are other reasons, too, for elevating your company's strategic IQ. In small companies, everyone's efforts are seriously important. If just one individual gets things wrong, they can sink you. In larger organizations, people without line of sight to the head office must constantly make up their own minds about how to act. They have to deal with suppliers, customers, and many other stakeholders. They're the public face of the organizations they represent. They need to know that in the eyes of outsiders, *they are the company*. And they need to know how to handle that responsibility.

Strategic IQ is too big an issue to be left to chance. It must be taken seriously and managed deliberately. Therefore, it should be a key item on the agenda of every leader (and definitely not a task delegated to the human resources department).

Expectations and performance

If you think Kerry in Accounts is both competent and a joy to deal with, you'll respect her views and be pleasant when you work with her. If you've made up your mind that Kevin in Sales is a devious bastard who never produces the goods, you'll be ultra-cautious with him and double-check everything he says.

Framing people is natural. By putting them in a box we can store them in our minds. Then, when we think "clever," we can haul out Paula or Dan; "dangerous" means Steve; "strategic thinker" means Susan. Or, when we bump into these folk, we can quickly decide whom we're dealing with.

But it does no one any favours when those boxes have labels with negative words on them – as they often do. We all live up to expectations. Making people feel inadequate or stupid makes them less than they could be. That means *your* leadership job just gets harder. (Nor do you have to come out and tell someone you think they're a dimwit. You send that signal in countless subtle and unconscious ways.)

Our world views are framed by everything that happens to us. Some events leave indelible marks. Others may be surpassed by what happens next. Nature endows us with part of our personality. "Nurture" shapes the rest.

Psychologists say we're most impressionable in the first four or five years of our lives. But we do have the capacity to learn and change. Many people undergo radical transformations as they mature. This possibility is an opportunity not to be missed.

The person or the place?

Time and again, I've heard executives say things like this:

"George is disruptive. Not a team player. He has to go."

"Pat can't sell. We have to get someone else."

"Debbie is bloody useless." (This can mean anything from "Lacks basic computer skills" to "Didn't get my coffee last Friday.")

Maybe these people *do* come up short or *have* failed to perform. But then, to everyone's surprise, they leave and do brilliantly somewhere else. So what happened? Was it the *person* or the *place* that made the difference? Did someone deliberately hire an incompetent misfit?

Not likely.

Since the only thing that changed was the place, that's where to look. Company A provided a context for failure; Company B inspires success. The leader in Company A must take the rap. The leader in Company B is a winner.

Many factors add up to making a high-performance workplace. The culture of an organization has a great impact on its competitiveness, so doing something about it seems to be the smart move. In fact, it's mostly a waste of time.

The culture trap

Since *In Search of Excellence* was published in 1982, culture has been a big thing in management. Tom Peters and Bob Waterman gave a previously obscure notion star quality.[41] Now, when a company nosedives, someone is sure to finger culture as the culprit. Whenever executives get together to talk strategy, someone's bound to say:

"This company's culture is rotten."

"If we don't get our culture right, we'll never crack that market."

"Our new plant will be up and running by June. Now we must fix the culture."

Statements like these are common in the corridors of power. They're made all the time, and often trigger a flurry of work. But while the diagnosis might be right, the cure is wrong. What follows is almost always confusion, waste, and frustration.

Change consultants love culture. It's a slippery concept that opens the door to a host of "interventions" such as psychometric testing, studies of group dynamics, team building, and performance management. So it keeps them busy for a long time and earns them fat fees.

Corporate executives are big fans too. They buy it all because it sounds sexy and they don't know what else to do. If everyone's talking about culture it must surely be The Problem and The Solution.

But there are a couple of hitches:

1. **Culture isn't conveniently visible.** You can't easily see it, so you can't easily describe a particular firm's culture. It's superficial and unhelpful to say,

"They're rooted in the past," "They have an engineering mindset," or "They have no idea what customer service means."

2. **Culture is an amalgam of deeply embedded assumptions, beliefs, values, and behaviours which has developed over time.** In a crisis, people might feel the need to change quite quickly, or you may be able to quickly replace a large number of key people. But mostly, changing culture is a long, slow slog.[42] It's brainless to imagine you can do it as easily as you can change a machine, a production process, or the layout of an office.

Extraordinary efforts have been made to change the culture in various companies around the world. The results are pitiful. Most of these projects fail. They're either dumped quickly in favour of the next new thing, or linger for ages. They consume time and energy, piss people off, and destroy trust and the credibility of management.

Culture continues to get undeserved attention. It's a favourite conference theme and the subject of any number of books, articles, and speeches. But as a tool for change, it's clumsy, costly, and potentially debilitating.

That said, let me be clear:

- Culture *exists*; it's a reality you have to deal with.
- It impacts directly and significantly on performance, and either improves your chances of success or gets in the way.
- If it's at odds with your purpose and you don't change it, your organization may never deliver different results.

Obviously, you should aim to foster a culture that will work for your business. But be rational. First, understand why efforts to change culture seldom work. There are many reasons, but two stand out:

1. **You don't change people's behaviour by changing their minds. You change their minds by changing their behaviour.** (Psychologists have known this for about 100 years. Executives still think you can ignore the facts.)
2. **The only person who can effectively champion change in an organization is the chief executive.** But because he's busy with weightier matters, the job

usually lands on the desk of the eager HR executive. She has no clout, even though the CEO says, "This vital project has my total support, and Carla has my full authority to make it happen."

Change on the run

All the evidence about what it takes to change organizations leads to a simple conclusion:

Leaders drive change by inspiring people to *do* new things fast.

Action in the short term changes hearts and minds in the long term. By focusing on what you *can* change today, you let your people learn what's possible tomorrow.

Try asking for a two per cent improvement in sales, productivity, or quality in the next 30 days. Then for another similar improvement the following month. And so on. In a year, you'll see major gains. What's more, if somehow you're able to assess your firm's culture today and again next year, you'll probably conclude, "This is a different place. What a culture shift!"

But recognize what changed the culture. (If you have to improve performance again, perhaps in another firm, you need to know what lever to pull.)

All you changed, really, was your expectations and the deadline. Those, in turn, stirred people to action. But if that's the start, it's not enough. To embed high performance in your company, you have to do more than merely present a challenge. You have to change the arena in which people work.

Climate for action

By contrast with culture, *climate* gets almost no air time. It's seldom a subject in management journals. There are few books on it, and it seldom appears in indexes. Yet an organization's climate is a core element in its performance. It has a profound impact on how people feel about their jobs, and therefore what they'll give to them.[43]

According to Manfred Kets De Vries, 70 per cent of executives blame "dysfunctional leadership" for their stress. The same percentage point to leadership as the reason why they leave organizations.[44] The climate that leaders create is a key reason for either good or bad performance.

When firms are struggling, their HR people often recommend climate studies to "take the temperature." Then they promptly set about trying to change the *culture*. Later, they take another climate reading to check how they're doing ... then get back to work on the culture.

Executives who understand the influence of climate are able to influence people surprisingly easily and without all the commotion caused by trying to change culture. The factors that influence climate are obvious:

- Direction
- Support
- Trust
- Respect
- Information
- Openness
- Integrity
- Stretch

Provide them, and you'll see these results:

- Performance
- Alignment
- Cooperation
- "Volunteerism"
- Respect
- Energy
- Integrity
- Stretch

Look at those two lists. See the common factors? *What you give, you get.*

Let's face it, this isn't complicated stuff. It's down-to-earth common sense. But perhaps because it is so simple, executives barely think about it. They expect great performance, but don't recognize that *they* create the conditions for it. With their minds on other things, they literally set their people up to fail. Then they curse them and call the headhunters. "Find some people who're hungry for challenges," they say. "People who can think for themselves, and who *want* to work."

And when they find them … they destroy them.

Magic in meaning

In all the animal kingdom, only humans have a psychological need for *meaning*. Only we are *self*-conscious. "Who am I?" is a question we struggle with continually. "Why do I exist?" is equally perplexing. Sometimes, we have our own answers. But no matter how sure we may be of them, no matter how confident we are about ourselves, we need the confirmation of others. They make us whole.[45] I am indeed my brother's keeper.

Work is an important source of meaning. It gets us up in the mornings and gives us purpose. We feel good when we're busy with significant challenges. We learn and grow in the process. But it's not just accomplishment that matters. The workplace is a rich social environment. It's where we spend most of our waking hours and where we mix with people, make friends, share information, brainstorm for ideas, argue, gossip – and hopefully also have fun.

Yet *all* work is not meaningful. "The mass of men," wrote Henry David Thoreau, more than 150 years ago in his famous book *Walden*, "lead lives of quiet desperation."[46] More recently, there have been many cases of workers saying, "They hired a whole person, then expected me to leave my brain at the gate."

Businesses are the most important units in society. But they're more than just the engine of the economy. They are also the arena in which people discover themselves. Leaders who grasp this second fact will achieve more than those who don't. This single insight can do more for your performance than almost any other. If you get up each day intent on creating an environment for greatness, you'll benefit more than you can imagine. You'll be surprised by what comes back to you.

Trust

With many forces tearing at them, organizations can easily fly apart. Trust is the glue that holds them together. When it's there, people are open and frank with each other, and their discourse is likely to be nourishing and therefore healthy. Without it, you have a climate in which toxic conversation is assured.

Trust is a fragile commodity. It's harder to build than destroy. Building it takes time, while destroying it takes a nanosecond.

I work with people at all levels of major organizations, and it's evident that those at the top see things very differently from the rest. They're big on trust. They talk about it often. In their own minds, they're straight shooters who hide nothing and always "tell it like it is," who deliver on their promises and never betray confidences.

But check how others see things. They'll tell you about assurances that came to nothing. About colleagues betrayed. About disappointments and dismay at the actions of those they admired. And about the double standards that exist in every area, allowing senior people and their favourites to get away with things that would get anyone else fired.

To hold people's trust over time is never easy. Human beings are fallible. Those in leadership roles are watched especially closely for signs of weakness or deceit. Sceptics are always nearby to finger them, to put their own spin on things, and to say, "I told you so."

Sometimes it's necessary to act in ways that will be seen as inconsistent. Sometimes you have to share less than you know or would like to reveal. And yes, the rules of the game do change – you may have to "zig" when you said you would only ever "zag."

But trust is not built in a vacuum. It always has a *context*. And often the reason for distrust is ignorance of the facts of a situation. So, if you leave people to make up their minds about why you act in a particular way, they'll do just that and you shouldn't curse them for it. On the other hand, if you ensure that they're fully informed, and if you explain your current actions in light of specific conditions, they're likely to cut you some slack.

Trust is not a one-way thing. Leaders expect it, but are slow to give it. But until you give it, you don't get it. Maybe this is a risk. But not to take it is a far greater risk. Without this powerful bond, deceit rules. You have to micro-manage everyone, control everything, and hang on for dear life.

3
On Being Effective

"*A monumental question for leaders in any organization to consider is: how much greatness are we willing to grant people?*"

Rosamund Stone Zander & Benjamin Zander, The Art of Possibility[47]

Your effectiveness as a leader isn't an accidental thing. You need to be clear in your own mind about what you aim to achieve, and why it matters. And you need to make that clear to others.

But that's only the start of the journey to high performance. The workplace is an arena for action, innovation, learning, sharing, and caring. In other words, for being fully human.

"The new world of work" is a fashionable notion. For a while, trends seemed to indicate that organizations as we know them would cease to exist. In their place, we'd see "virtual organizations," along with a boom in "hotelling," "telecommuting," "portfolio careers," and the like. In fact, today's organizations are much like yesterday's. Little will change tomorrow. People will still have to work together because they get more done that way than on their own. They'll be motivated by the same things that turn them on now. They'll have roughly the same values, expectations, and needs. Currently sound practices will endure.

Sure, there might be more women at work, and they'll need maternity leave and help with child care. There will be more laws about health and safety. And the norms for every step between recruitment and retirement (or retrenchment or firing) will change. But the basics of good management will stay the same.

The fact is, we know what works, and have done for years. There's very little new in management. The "best practices" are all underpinned by respect, listening, trust, compassion, and integrity, and this won't change. You can bury those words in fashionable theories, but you can't deny them. They're the core of leadership excellence. All else is puffery.

Action on purpose

A great deal of the activity in any organization "just happens." There's no good reason for it. It is, literally, without purpose.

When leaders allow too much of this to occur, their organizations either fly apart or atrophy. Their people have no good reason to apply themselves, and no incentive to stretch. Work becomes a tedious chore. There's no point in being innovative. People do just enough not to get noticed. They fill their time reading, gossiping, or taking long coffee or lunch breaks. Absenteeism becomes a problem. Workplace accidents and injuries rise. Staff turnover increases.

The flip side of this costly reality is that people in many firms, for no apparent good reason, make the most extraordinary efforts to produce results. They're the *volunteers* every leader should want beside her. But they make their efforts in a vacuum.

Without a larger purpose, they have to energize themselves. Without a leader reminding them where they should aim, their efforts aren't coordinated or aligned. Without meaning in their work, they drown themselves in meaningless activities.

If a firm has specific goals, it follows that its people should devote most of their imagination and energy towards achieving those goals. This won't happen just because everyone knows it should. Nor will some "self-organizing" principle make it happen (as the chaos theorists would have us believe.) On the contrary: the only things leaderless organizations can be sure of are *dis*organization, sloth, and premature death.

"The hill"

If you expect to deliver results through others, you have to make clear what results you seek. You have to spell out your end goal – "That's the hill we're aiming at" – and keep attention focused on it. Purposeful work is more productive and more satisfying than mindless striving.

When people aren't sure where you're headed, you have to control and monitor them all the time, or they'll stray off course. By contrast, when they know your intentions, you can set them free to invent their own way to the future. Clarity *energizes* your organization; vagueness *enervates* it.

Vision is a natural topic in any conversation about leadership. We feel comfortable when we think our leaders have it, and uneasy when they don't. (Remember when George Bush senior didn't get "the vision thing"? He was lampooned. The comment cost him lots of political points and will be linked to his name forever. Or remember what happened just after Louis Gerstner was appointed chairman and CEO of IBM, when he said, "The last thing this company needs is another vision"? The investment community went nuts. Big Blue was in crisis, and the leader had no vision!)

Surveys by Bain & Company show vision and mission to be among the most popular of all management tools.[48] Yet if you ask top executives to tell you what their meticulously crafted vision and mission statements say, they usually can't tell you. This makes the "tools" worthless and the effort to use them futile.

"Vision" and "mission" mean quite different things.* In my early years as a consultant, I used to labour mightily to get executives to understand the difference between them. We'd spend hours debating the words that would give their firms an edge. It was a pointless exercise. Vision and mission were always confused with each other. Most of the statements that followed were mush – and interchangeable with those of other firms!

Today, I get my clients to think about their *purpose* – "Why does our firm exist?" – rather than their vision and mission. It's a crisp and focused concept, but it invariably inspires a richer debate. It also kills the possibility of confusion ("Are we talking vision now, or mission?") Not surprisingly, it is a concept that is gaining popularity around the world.

To explain your "hill" to people, you probably need no more than a handful of words, a few bullet points, or maybe a simple picture. Anything more means that

---

* Vision describes your end goal. Mission describes which customers you'll aim for, what you'll sell, and how you'll do it.

you haven't thought through what you intend doing, and is bound to confuse people. So "keep it simple, stupid!" You'll make everyone smarter that way.

Remember, though, that while pinpointing "true north" may be a key factor in making your organization effective, it is only a start. Besides, obsession with a distant goal – "The technology leader by 2010," "30 per cent growth per year," "Own the market" – can have precisely the effect you seek to avoid. Instead of inspiring great performance, it can actually ensure *mediocre* performance.

The reason is that you don't get from here to there in one effortless leap. There's always hard work between you and your goals, and it may be boring, to boot. You have to take lots of small steps and build capabilities as you go. It's an ongoing struggle to keep your team focused on the task at hand and motivated to produce short-term results. And when the long-term goal stays "out there" and they get the feeling that it's all just a silly dream, they can become angry and disillusioned.

To make your intentions reality, you have to keep promoting them. You have to keep telling the story of why your purpose matters and how you'll attain it. You have to make it meaningful to everyone on your team, and you have to help every individual see how he or she can make it happen.

Your point of view

Leaders fail for many reasons. Among the most obvious ones are these:
- They make dumb assumptions about markets.
- They make ill-judged decisions.
- They can't get the resources they need.
- They fail to win support for their ventures.
- They let controls slip.
- Their execution is poor.

But there's another reason that looms above all of these. It impacts on everything else. Its cost is immeasurable. Yet it gets almost no attention. The culprit:

The leader has no clear point of view.

Partly, this is about setting direction. That, after all, is what people expect of their leaders. They need to know where to focus their efforts. But there's more.

Leaders need a point of view so they can explain the "*why*." Staying with the "what" and the "how," no matter how well explained, won't inspire anyone. They'll always have a sense that something's missing.

A leader's point of view is more than direction. It's also an expression of her values: "I believe this is what we must do, *because* ...." So it comes partly from rational thinking, and largely from personal character and deep, intro-spective thought.

Watch people in conversation – and particularly when things get sticky. Many will duck and dive and change their tune to suit whomever they're talking to. One minute they believe this, the next they believe that. If the heat rises and an argument develops, they dig in and get dogmatic. Because they believe in nothing, they'll defend anything.

Changing your mind is perfectly normal and healthy. It's the smart thing to do if you have new information. It shows your willingness to listen, and your flexi-bility. But constantly shifting your ground to appease others or prove them wrong is stupid. It merely highlights your uncertainty. That, in turn, makes *them* unsure. After all, if you give way on this matter now, how can anyone ever believe you?

If beliefs aren't worth defending, they're probably not worth expressing. If you can't back them with reasonable arguments, perhaps you should rethink them. To lay them out to view and then argue for them does nothing for your credibility. Nor does it advance the conversation.

(From time to time, however, you want to "fly a trial balloon" to provoke dis-cussion and to get a sense of what others think. But when you do this, you need to quite rapidly reveal your true position. Your timing is critical. Switch too soon, and the debate might peter out. But wait too long, and you'll dig a hole for yourself.)

Arriving at your point of view on any matter can be a tortuous process. It begins with surfacing ideas in your own mind, and evaluating them as honestly as you can. You also need to test them "in the court of public opinion," where other people with different views can challenge your thinking. Conversations about the business environment, strategy, and operational matters all offer a chance to do this.

Ground rules

If your people are to be effective, they need to know what you expect of them. They need to know what behaviours you'll reward, what you'll tolerate, and what's unacceptable. If you don't provide this understanding, you leave it up to them to decide what's appropriate. Mostly, they'll be able to work this out for themselves. But not always. On occasion, things will come unstuck. And, as the saying goes, one bad apple can spoil the whole barrel.

Most firms today have a set of values. Often, these have been well publicized on posters and pocket cards and in speeches and videos. Yet many people don't get the message. Ask them, "What counts around here?" and you get answers like these:

- "The boss doesn't like surprises."
- "Don't be the bearer of bad news."
- "Make the numbers – even if you have to make them up."
- "Keep something in your bottom drawer just in case they ask for more."
- "Never mention competitors by name."
- "Fill in everything on your expense sheets, even if you lie, or Accounting will go nuts."

While these are hardly what you want people to say, they reflect the reality of organizational life. People aren't stupid. They soon learn what it takes to survive in any company. The climate you shape will either encourage openness and honesty, or deviousness and cover-ups.

In helping executives think about the organizations they want to create, I encourage them to go beyond a simple list of values to a deeper debate about the organization's *character*. They agree on "Who we are" when they ask and answer tough questions:

"What assumptions underpin our behaviour?"

"What turns us on?"

"What's not negotiable?"

"What behaviours do we value?"[49]

This gives a more complete picture of the ground rules that matter than does a mere statement of values. It tests both the results people want and the reasoning behind them. (Remember how your parents drove you crazy when they justified themselves by saying, "Because *I* said so ...."? The same thing happens when adults don't understand things!)

When you've got your ground rules figured out, you still face the challenge of communicating them. Never assume you've got your message through to people. If you don't keep repeating it, in various forums and in various ways, they'll forget or ignore it.

The only way to show you're serious is:
- Keep your list of ground rules short.
- Explain them carefully.
- Emphasize them in the context of real work.
- Keep talking.

In other words, use your rules whenever you discuss strategy or processes, or review results. This way, they become meaningful and people can connect them to their jobs.

Four modes of operating

The work of leaders is all about *influence*. Sometimes, it's about pointing people in a certain direction, and pushing them for specific results. At other times, it's about inspiring them to think, to imagine new possibilities, and to create novel solutions to problems. With one person, instructions may be necessary; you need to guide them carefully and be specific about priorities, methods, tools, and so on. With another, you'll do best by defining the goal, then standing back and letting them get on with it. Adaptability and flexibility are always better than a rigid approach.

But, that said, it's a fact that most human beings are pretty inflexible. We all have preferred modes of operating.

When we deal with others, we feel most comfortable either *telling* them stuff or *listening* to them. And we tend to use either *logic* or *emotion* to make our point or win their support (Figure 3-1). Of course, we don't stick rigidly to these patterns, but we do have "comfort zones." Knowing where we feel at ease helps us see ourselves as others see us; it also helps us see possibilities for change – and for enhanced performance.

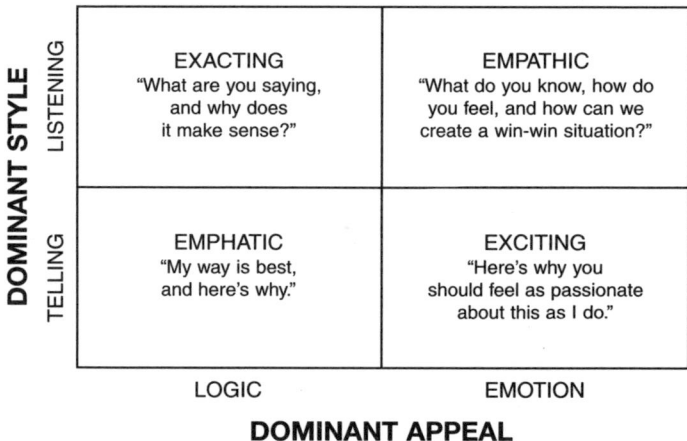

Figure 3-1: *Operating modes*

1. **Emphatic – "My way is best, and here's why."** If this is you, you're a poor listener. You're convinced that your point of view is the right one. You use logic – facts, figures, structured argument – to sell what you have to say. You're so compelling that other people might find it hard to argue. Whether

they buy your line or not, they feel that going along with you is the wise thing to do.

2. **Exacting – "What are you saying, and why does it make sense?"** People in this mode are excellent listeners. But they're more alert to the logic in what people say than to their feelings. They question and probe rigorously, testing assumptions, checking facts, digging for "the truth." It can be very uncomfortable being interrogated by these folks, but at least you have your say. (Just get your story *right!*)

3. **Exciting – "I'm passionate about this; you should be too!"** These tub-thumpers are sure they're right, and hyped up about doing what they do. They expect everyone else to feel the same. They're evangelists on a mission. Their enthusiasm can often swing the mob their way. But because they try to make things happen through sheer exuberance, they may win immediate support then lose it almost as fast.

4. **Empathic – "What do *you* know, how do *you* feel, and how can *we* create a win-win situation?"** In this mode, you look beyond logic and tune in to other people's deepest feelings. When you get onto their wavelength, you understand what turns them on or off. Because they sense that you care, they're likely to reciprocate by agreeing with you.

Each of these styles is effective in different circumstances. Although one of them will be natural for you, failing to use *all* of them limits your ability to get through to others.

Remember, though, that communication is a two-way exchange. It only happens when people's emotions connect and when they share meaning. Anything else is just noise. And just as you have your preferred style, so does everyone else.

Only by listening deeply to the feelings of others, and adapting your communication style to suit the moment, can you hope to connect with them. Only by walking in their shoes can you know how to say what you want them to hear.

Making your point may be critical, but it's not the whole story. Without support for it, all is lost.

The second right answer

Under pressure to clear items off your agenda, solve every problem "right now," and demonstrate your decisiveness, you might be tempted to race for answers. Your example can spread the habit throughout your organization. "Ready, fire, aim" can become a corporate battle cry.

Many firms would gain mightily if this were to happen. Plagued by analysis paralysis, what they need most is a call to action. Doing something – *anything*, in many cases – is better than doing nothing. More information doesn't always lead to better decisions. Often it just slows things down and leads to confusion. Besides, you only learn when you act.

However, the first "right" decision is often not the best one. Here's why:

1. In your haste to get there fast, you might arrive *too* fast, without considering all relevant factors.

2. Even the most carefully made decisions often benefit from a bit of "soaking." They get better with age. Besides, if you allow them time, ideas spawn other ideas.

3. What looks like the best decision today might look wrong tomorrow or next week. Things change, or you might come up with a better answer.

In a wonderful little book called *Zen in the Art of Archery*, the Master tells his pupil, "What stands in your way is that you have too much wilful will. You think that what you do not do yourself does not happen." The cure? "You must learn to wait properly …. by letting go of yourself, leaving yourself and everything yours behind you so decisively that nothing more is left of you but a purposeless tension."[50]

Leaders must produce action. Speed is a valuable competitive weapon. Our hyperkinetic society leads us to believe that all action must occur right now. Yet the frenetic behaviour so characteristic of this age flies in the face of reality. Doing things faster must be a goal. But knowing when to do *nothing* is a supreme act of judgment.

Second-guessing yourself is never a good idea. But it's smart to ask, "What else could we do?" ... "How would someone else deal with this?" ... "Is there a better way?"

Ideas can be end points or stepping stones. When you have to call time out and take action, do it. But when you can afford to develop alternatives, then rather do that. The worst that will happen is that you'll agree with yourself that your first idea was the right one.

The finite resource

All of us have 24 hours a day in which to do our thing. How you use that time makes you either ordinary or a star. You either get the right things done or leave too many of them undone. It's as simple as that.

Workers on a factory floor have narrow agendas. They operate machines or maintain things. They don't need to worry about what's happening next door in the tool shop or over in Sales or Administration. Further up the ladder, agendas start to expand. At the top, they explode.

Running a business of any size is a complicated job. Running a major corporation is the stuff of nightmares. Everyone's problems are important and they're all urgent. Nothing can wait. The lobbying and the pressures are incessant. If you're not tough, you get swamped. So you need to apply this discipline:

Step 1. Make up your own mind how you should spend your time.

Step 2. Balance your time between external and internal matters.

Step 3. Be 100 per cent disciplined about doing only what you and you alone should do, and hand the rest to other people.

Step 4. Constantly review your "to do" list and lop off anything you haven't made progress on in the past week, or anything you can't start on in the next 48 hours.

Step 5. Accept that some things that seem desperately important will go away if you just ignore them.

Before deciding whether to dive in and dirty your hands or stand back and let others get on with it, you might ask:

- Will taking charge of the action be the best use of my time?
- Am I really the best person to make the critical things happen?
- What signals will I send by taking that role?
- Will I get the support I need?
- Who might I lose, and how might that matter?
- If things go right, how will my team benefit?
- If things go wrong, what are the consequences?
- What happens to my other responsibilities while I'm busy with this?
- Instead of spending time here, what else might I more usefully do?

Time management is common sense. It's not hard to know what belongs on your agenda and what doesn't. The trouble is, we all like to look important and busy. We assume that other people are idiots and only we can get things done. We're easily suckered by their agendas, pleading, and pressure. And we cave in especially fast when they're powerful, rich, or attractive.

Being helpful, kind, and polite all count in your favour in your relationships. At work, they're also the means to the end of achieving specific results through others – and that's what goes on the scoreboard.

Leaders as teachers

The 1990s saw executives striving to make their firms "learning organizations." That hasn't worked very well. The new decade will see a sharp swing. The new trend: "*teaching* organizations."

Organizational learning is a largely passive process. Most of it happens by *default* rather than intentionally. Most of the learning that does take place is *personal* learning. Most is *private* rather than shared. Lots of information flies about in any company, but people generally hog what hits them. (After all, knowledge is power; intellectual capital is a tradable commodity. If you've made the effort to learn something – or discovered it by accident – why give other people the advantage?)

Organizational teaching is an active, deliberate process. It's not left to personal choice or to chance. The goals are clear and the curriculum and content are carefully designed. Almost anything that happens to the firm or in it can be used as teaching material.

The head teachers in any organization are its leaders. It's their responsibility to ensure that people learn the right things. If you leave that task to someone else, don't be surprised if they get the syllabus wrong and screw up on delivery.

Leading is teaching. Not the "pedagogical" teaching of most primary school classrooms, but rather the "andragogical" teaching of, say, a business school class.* When you ask people to describe their richest learning experiences, they'll seldom say, "Being lectured to." What does make a difference is:

- Having fun.
- Being involved in solving an important problem.
- Listening/observing.
- Emotional events (e.g. personal tragedy).
- Information presented in an interesting way.
- Reflecting on an experience.
- Doing things.

The message to leaders who see the need to be teachers is simple: Don't preach. Your people are a rich resource. *Much of what you want your team to learn is probably in their heads already.* You'll bring it to the surface by questioning, challenging, and listening.

So take a risk. Display your ignorance and show you're open to learning. Dare to let people challenge your assumptions, ideas, and decisions. Encourage them to question things, not in a negative way, but to test the robustness of assumptions and logic. Provoke them to debate vigorously, so that they don't accept the arguments they hear too quickly.

---

* "Pedagogical" comes from the Greek *child*, and refers to the method where the teacher is the resource and tells children about a subject; 'andragogical' comes from *adult*, and refers to a collaborative learning experience, where all participants are resources, and the teacher is the facilitator of their learning adventure.

Even apparently average people bring an enormous amount of knowledge to work. Every day, they add to that store in the process of doing their jobs and going about their private lives. Their imagination is infinite. Your challenge as a leader is to make *explicit* what they know *implicitly*. To bring to the surface what's buried in their brains.

This only happens when you make it known that speaking up is OK, and that saying foolish things is key to producing breakthrough ideas. It happens when, over time, you create a climate in which people are rigorously challenged so that they have to think about what they're saying. And when they learn that their opinions matter, and that they can make a difference.

Lifelong learning

Leaders also need to think about their own learning, for this is the resource they must call upon constantly in order to be successful.

It's been said that the half-life of an executive's knowledge today is five or six years. What you know becomes rapidly dated and possibly useless. If you don't keep re-tooling your mind, you'll fall behind. Yet many top executives are surprisingly uninterested in what's happening around them. They don't deliberately expose themselves to new information, they're not curious, and they don't readily change their minds.

Learning takes place continuously. Much of it is subconscious. We don't know it's happening, nor do we know *what* we've learned.

What's more, says Harvard professor Chris Argyris, most of our learning is of the "single-loop" type: "X happened, so Y is the result." Without some effort, "double-loop" learning – "X happened, so Y is the result, but what's the *underlying cause* of X?" – is unlikely.[51] Through single-loop learning, we at best understand cause-effect relationships. Double-loop learning, on the other hand, also lets us understand the "why."

To overcome these problems, you need to become more aware of your learning. You'll do so when you make a habit of asking these questions:

- *What* am I learning about?
- What have I learned about that *subject*?
- What have I learned about *myself*?
- What have I learned about *learning*?

Like most things, learning is a matter of practice. The more you do it, the better you get. The more you talk about it in your organization, the more likely others will be to take responsibility for their own learning and growth.

Pause to reflect

In the hustle and bustle of daily life, most things pass by us without sticking. We may experience a lot, but we learn relatively little.

If you want proof, just think back to the last conversation you had. Let's assume you can remember some of what the other person or people said. Now, what did you *learn*? Probably nothing. The instant that conversation was over, you shut the door (your mind) on it and moved on to something else.

A lot of what happens in any firm provides an opportunity for learning. If people became more conscious of this, and if they asked the questions I've suggested, they'd be able to use new information and insights more effectively. And if they shared their learning with each other, the impact on the "strategic IQ" of their organizations would be immense.

Few companies can be called learning organizations, simply because they're not *reflecting* organizations. Busy-ness rules. There's too much to do. People have no time to pause and think about what just happened. They rush frantically from one task to the next. The problem gets worse when there's pressure on costs and jobs are cut. Yet that's precisely when companies need to use their learning well.

Without reflection, change is often impossible. At best, people do new things without being convinced of the "why," or sure that they have the best way. So make reflection a regular practice in your company. Allow time for it to happen, and make it deliberate. Build time for it into meetings and reviews.

And make sure that you reflect on what *worked* as well as what *didn't,* on *positive* experiences as well as *negative* ones. You never know where your next great idea might come from.

4
TOMORROW'S LEADERS

"Each man is a hero and an oracle to somebody."

Ralph Waldo Emerson

The organization with the best team wins. The leader's most important task is to create an organization that works. There are three key elements:
1. Defining the organization's purpose.
2. Appointing the right people.
3. Creating a climate for high performance.

What about strategy, structure, resources, processes, technology, and all the other stuff of so much debate and concern? All important, of course. But first comes the "engine." Get that right and many other things fall into place. Get it wrong, and everything becomes an issue.

Since we've already talked about purpose and climate, let's focus now on the central issue: people. On identifying and growing the leaders of the future.

Insiders or outsiders?

Some CEOs get their jobs the old-fashioned way: by working through the ranks over a long period. But a growing number are headhunted and parachuted in to deal with a crisis.

"New blood" is often seen as the only answer to a slide in performance. In many cases this cure is right. People already in the system can be part of the problem. Even though they "get religion" and say the right things about change, they may lack the *credibility* to get it done. Their skills, too, may be deficient.

(Cynics say a major reason outsiders are so often brought in is that head-hunters earn their big fees by promoting the practice. They're aided and abetted by boards of directors who feel they need to send a powerful signal to the market. Both factors obviously do have influence.)

There are good reasons why insiders are likely to be the most successful leaders.[52] They've "been around the block" with their firms. Their "corporate memory" is invaluable. They understand the company "code" and the industry practices and players. They know what happened when deals were done in the past and when new initiatives were tried. They know how things work (and where the skeletons are).

By now everyone agrees that people are a company's most valuable resource. They also agree that knowledge is the one asset worth anything in the long run – and this is the age of "empowerment," "learning organizations," and "intellectual capital." So there are compelling reasons to promote from within, to encourage long tenure, and to give leaders time to do their thing.

But there are equally compelling reasons to take the opposite view. Fresh thinking is the best antidote to a stale culture. Outsiders challenge what insiders take for granted. They kill sacred cows. They show that there are different ways to see things, to think, and to act. They're a breath of fresh air in stultified organizations.

What's more, leaders who come from outside usually find it easier to make radical changes. They're *hired to make changes*. They're not part of whatever problems exist. They have no outstanding IOUs in their new organization, and neither they nor their partners or spouses* are tied by old bonds of friendship.

Selecting against the odds

Picking the right person for a leadership job is fraught with risks. No matter how carefully you go about it, there's always a chance that:

---

* The "spouse factor" is often the biggest one in determining personal and corporate performance. There's a partner behind most people, to whom things must be explained and justified. They have their own opinions, and can be enormously powerful.

1. You get the wrong person.
2. The person you select has the right stuff, but doesn't perform in their new role.
3. They produce *some* important results, but in the process do serious harm to your company's long-term prospects. (For example, they cut costs, gain market share, and improve profits – but they also drive out key people, alienate suppliers, behave unethically, or poison government relationships.)

However, you can take some of the uncertainty out of the process. Here are some steps that help make it more deliberate and less accidental. They apply equally whether you're promoting someone from inside your organization or looking for an outsider.

1. **Get enough candidates.** This needs saying because too often it's a one-horse race. A single individual stands out so clearly that no one else is even considered. They may be a Rhodes Scholar, the daughter of the founder, a special friend, or have a fine track record. It doesn't matter why they're The Candidate (though some reasons may give more cause for concern than others). What does matter is that there's no other choice. This is bad for the person, bad for the people around them, and bad for the organization.

   A favourite gets favouritism. Instead of being tested, they get an easy ride. They're the benchmark, so they set the standard. "We give them a hard time *because* they're the favourite" is nonsense. For one thing, it's probably not true. Then, it discounts the fact that favourites also get invitations to lunch in the executive dining room, access to information, the benefit of important social contacts, plus a whole lot more. These taken-for-granted benefits are invaluable. They fast-track the candidate's learning and experience. They also expose him to people likely to *confirm* that he's the right choice. (No one says after lunch with the chairman, "Young Jeffrey is the dumbest person I ever met. What on earth is he doing here?" More likely, they say, "Wonderful young man, Jeffrey. Remarkable intelligence. I can see why you've got him marked for bigger things.")

2. **Define the job.** This goes without saying. But often the definition isn't helpful. As a consultant, I'm often in on the decision to appoint a new leader. Inevitably,

platitudes like "visionary" and "lateral thinker" are trotted out to describe the person to be sought. But this Pavlovian response (vision = leadership) is horribly narrow-minded. Are those really the characteristics to look for? How do you see them or know them? What else matters … maybe even more?

Because appointing a leader is often a sensitive matter, few people are involved and fewer still know the details. The job definition may be spelled out by the board director handling the assignment. Then it's fine-tuned by a senior HR executive before being handed to a search consultant.

This small band brings a very narrow view to defining who'll be best for the job. They'd do well to solicit opinions from around the organization, because other people would see things in different ways. They're in tune with what's going on both inside and outside the firm. They know how things work. They have views about what the new person should do. They know the strengths and weaknesses of the person being replaced. But most important of all, by making the new hire *"their* choice," you ease the stranger's way into the organization.

3. **Cast your net wide.** On the surface, it might seem best to appoint someone with experience in your industry, or from a firm similar to yours. But what about an outsider with a different point of view? What about someone from a totally different industry? From a much smaller or much bigger company? With "too little" experience? With no formal education?

    Do you automatically disqualify them? Or do you put them on your list and start talking to find out what they might bring to the party?

    As I've stressed throughout this book, leadership is a mysterious thing. It's too easy to disqualify people on the basis of "shortcomings" that mean little or nothing. And given the "war for talent," surely there's a case for opening your mind to the possibilities in unlikely people, rather than automatically shutting them out.

4. **Be methodical.** Despite what I said in that last section, recruitment shouldn't be a slapdash process. The more you understand about your candidate up front, the better. To find out about their shortcomings after they're appointed is both costly and inconvenient, to say the least.

Questionnaires, psychometric tests, and interviews will give you hard information and useful insights. Entertaining the candidate will give you some idea of their social graces. Meeting their spouses and families provides more clues. And of course, background checks are essential, as they provide other people's perspectives as well as validation of what the candidate has told you. (This is particularly important because a large proportion of people lie about themselves when they look for jobs!)

Your research should help you learn a lot about three areas of their make-up: their *job-related strengths*, their *personal needs and ambitions*, and their *character*. But don't be fooled. Although there are countless consultants with sure-fire methodologies, and more "predictive tools" than you can imagine, there's no perfect way to pick the right person.

The truth about anyone's capabilities and potential comes out over time. In theory, their past performance should tell you how they'll do in future. But don't bank on it. The archives of business are jammed with tales of men and women who were outstanding in one place and failed in the next.

Usually the criteria for a new leader are obvious. You can write your needs into a job description and tick them off as you get to know your candidate. But finally, you have to rely on personal "chemistry" and gut feel. Then, you have to toss your favoured person in at the deep end to see if they can swim.

5. **Allow "soaking" and "sweating" time.** Patience is a great virtue when you're trying to make up your mind about a key appointment. In the heat of the moment, you might be tempted to get the contract signed, make the announcement, and crack open the champagne. But wait.

Give yourself time to reflect on the person you've chosen. Give them time to think about it too. If either of you has second thoughts, best they surface now.

Make them sweat a bit. Even if you've indicated that they're your preferred candidate, let them see you're being ultra-careful. If they call to check how you're doing with your decision, use the opportunity to learn more about them. How badly do they want this job? *Why* do they want it so badly? Have they told you all you need to know? Are they still saying what they told you earlier?

An individual's fitness for any job hinges on many things. But the big question, when evaluating someone's leadership potential, is:

Can this person build an effective, robust organization?

If everything you know suggests that they can, then appoint them. If you have doubts, think again. The right person can make an astonishing difference. The wrong one can destroy a company.

Settling in

The appointment of a new leader is always an unsettling event. Even if he's well known to those he'll lead, and even if they're confident in his abilities, they don't know for sure that he'll perform, or how he'll operate.

Close personal ties between two people don't necessarily hold when one of them is promoted. Power changes things. A new leader has new agendas, challenges, and pressures. He has to move in different circles. His old buddies get left behind.

Getting to grips with a new role takes time. The new person has to learn many things, from where the toilet is to who really controls resources, wields influence, makes things happen, or gets in the way. So if you're appointing someone, be sure to allow them enough time. And if *you're* that someone, make sure you get the time you need. (This might not be possible in a crisis, but not every firm is in crisis.)

For a new leader, support is a vital commodity. The quicker you get it, the sooner you'll be able to show what you're worth. So in your early days, go out of your way to win votes. You're going to need them.

Decision time!

As we've seen throughout this book, leadership is a tough role. Even experienced people need the stamp of authority when they take up a new job. If they're the CEO, they need it from the Board. If they're heading a function, a division, a department, or whatever, they need it from the highest possible executive level. If you fail to signal that they're really, really important, you short-change them right from the start.

If you don't give this assurance to the people who're with you today, you have two choices:

1. Do it.
2. Replace them.

In both cases, I mean *right away*. Don't mess around.

To keep people on your team and set them up for failure is inexcusable. So make up your mind to make them great, or get them out fast.

But be honest. Consider carefully why they don't meet your expectations. Is it a question of skill … compatibility … integrity … teamwork … or what? And when did the specific issue become a problem to you? And what might have triggered it?

You can't build tomorrow's leaders by hacking carelessly at today's organization. It's a long, slow, frustrating process. You have to accept that you'll probably never get everyone you want on your team. Some people will shine, while others will have to be shoved. But it's your ability to inspire the magic in all of them that matters.

If you wish to be known as a leader, act the part and do what it takes. If you can't, make way for someone else. This is no time to seek power, fame, or wealth at the expense of humankind.

CONCLUSION

Few firms are basket cases. Most have the potential to perform far better than they do. Leadership is the key to new results.

While leadership is a hot topic, few people are clear about what it really is. Fewer still know what it takes. And as to developing leaders – well, that's mostly a joke.

There are lots of theories about leadership, but few basic principles. These principles are frequently overlooked in the search for some new "solution." But if firms – and individuals – simply started applying what's already well known, they'd save a lot of time and money, avoid a lot of frustration, and get the results they want.

In *Discovering the Essence of Leadership*, I've emphasized the factors that lead to success. But let's end with a look at some more reasons why leaders fail:

1. Leadership is many things, but mostly it's *message-making*. Few leaders understand this. Most are lousy message makers. Their messages are badly conceived, badly delivered, and changed too often.

2. Many people in leadership roles are unsure about themselves, unsure where they're taking their firms, and unsure about how to do it.[53] Lacking confidence, they can't confidently guide others.

3. They talk about the value of people and their "intellectual capital." They boast about their commitment to empowerment and training. But they treat people as a nuisance and a variable cost (using retrenchment as a way to quickly adjust their firms' capacity when market conditions change).

4. They blame their people's weaknesses for all their problems. Yet when you talk to their people, you find that *the leader* is the problem.

5. They're great talkers. But they don't always "walk their talk." They have one set of rules for themselves, and another for everyone else.

6. They like to think their work is "high-level stuff." Yet results come from mundane, "low-level" work. Many leaders are not good at getting the right things done.

Common sense, you say? Of course. But that, after all, is the essence of leadership.

THE PRACTICES

1. Manage the context.

2. Keep things simple.

3. Focus on the big picture / manage the basics.

4. Expect the extraordinary.

5. Encourage the unexpected.

6. Set bold, high-payoff goals / tight deadlines.

7. Share responsibility / demand accountability.

8. Be decisive / act fast.

9. Hold frequent, robust reviews, and give "rich," respectful feedback.

10. Communicate clearly, consistently and continually.

And finally,

Calm down ... and hurry up!

REFERENCES

1   Thomas A. Stewart, Alex Taylor III, Peter Petre and Brent Schlender, "The Businessman of the Century," *Fortune*, 22 November 1999

2   Tony Manning, *Making Sense of Strategy*, Cape Town: Zebra Press 2001; New York: Amacom 2002

3   John P. Kotter, *What Leaders Really Do*, Boston: Harvard Business School Press 1999

4   Fons Trompenaars and Charles Hampden-Turner, *21 Leaders For The 21st Century*, New York: McGraw-Hill 2002

5   Abraham Zaleznik, "Managers and Leaders: Are They Different," *Harvard Business Review*, May–June 1997

6   Warren Bennis and Burt Nanus, *Leaders*, New York: Harper & Row 1985

7   "Personal Histories," *Harvard Business Review*, December 2001

8   Jim Collins, *Good To Great*, New York: HarperCollins 2001

9   *King II Report*, Johannesburg: Institute of Directors of Southern Africa 2002

10   Robert S. Kaplan and David P. Norton, *The Balanced Scorecard*, Boston: Harvard Business School Press 1996

11   Robert G. Eccles, Robert H. Herz, E. Mary Keegan, and David M.H. Phillips, *The Value Reporting Revolution*, New York: John Wiley & Sons 2001

12   www.fortune.com/mostadmired

13   Douglas McGregor, *The Human Side of Enterprise*, New York: McGraw-Hill 1960

14   Carl Rogers, *On Becoming a Person*, London: Constable 1961

15   John P. Kotter, *The New Rules*, New York: The Free Press 1995

16   Willie Pietersen, *Reinventing Strategy*, New York: John Wiley & Sons 2002

17   Robert G. Eccles and Nitin Nohria, *Beyond The Hype*, Boston: Harvard Business School Press 1992

18   Abraham Zaleznik, "Managers and Leaders".

19   Al Senter, "Born to Run?" *Director*, January 2002

20   Paddy Miller, *Mission Critical Leadership*, London: McGraw-Hill 2001

21   "The CEO Trap," *Business Week*, 11 December 2000

22 "Churning at the top," *The Economist*, 15 March 2001

23 "Fallen idols," *The Economist*, 4 May 2002

24 Arie De Geus, *The Living Company*, Boston: Harvard Business School Press 1999

25 *Fortune*, 5 February 2001

26 Berkshire Hathaway annual report, 2001

27 Warren Bennis and James O'Toole, "Don't Hire The Wrong CEO," *Harvard Business Review*, May–June 2000

28 David McClelland, *The Achieving Society*, New York: D. Van Nostrand Co. 1961

29 "Cisco chief sees opportunities in downturn," *Financial Times*, 20 April 2001

30 "Bernie Ebbers, King of the WorldCom," *Time Digital* 50, 1999

31 Andy Kessler, "Bernie Bites the dust," *The Wall Street Journal Europe*, 1 May 2002

32 Alex Taylor III, "Crunch time for Jac," *Fortune*, 25 June 2001

33 "Yesterday's man," *The Economist*, 2 May 2002

34 John McCarthy, "Campaign Interview: Bill Bernbach," *Campaign*, 7 February 1969

35 Abraham H. Maslow, *The Farther Reaches of Human Nature*, New York: The Viking Press 1971

36 James Waldroop and Timothy Butler, *Maximum Success*, New York: Currency/Doubleday 2000

37 Laurence J. Peter and Raymond Hull, *The Peter Principle*, New York: William Morrow & Co 1969

38 Tony Manning, *Making Sense of Strategy*

39 Daniel Goleman, Richard Boyatzis, and Annie McKee, "Primal Leadership," *Harvard Business Review*, December 2001

40 See the General Electric annual report 2001

41 Thomas J. Peters and Robert H. Waterman, Jr., *In Search of Excellence*, New York: Harper & Row, 1982

42 Diane L. Coutu, "The Anxiety of Learning," an interview with Edgar H. Schein, *Harvard Business Review*, March 2002

43 Charles A. O'Reilly III and Jeffrey Pfeffer, *Hidden Value*, Boston: Harvard Business School Press 2000

44 Manfred Kets De Vries, *The Leadership Mystique*, London: Financial Times Prentice Hall 2001

45 Maslow, *The Farther Reaches of Human Nature*

46 Henry David Thoreau, *Walden*, 1854

47 Rosamund Stone Zander and Benjamin Zander, *The Art of Possibility*, Boston: Harvard Business School Press 2000

48 Bain & Company survey of management tools, 2002

49 Tony Manning, *Making Sense of Strategy*

50 Eugen Herrigel, *Zen in the Art of Archery*, London: Routledge & Kegan Paul 1953

51 Chris Argyris, *Knowledge For Action*, San Francisco: Jossey-Bass Publishers 1993

52 Jim Collins, *Good To Great*

53 Peter F. Drucker, "The theory of the business," *Harvard Business Review*, September–October, 1994